CONTENTS

I0594296

OZ TALES

PRESENTS

SHORT STORIES OF FOREST AND FANTASY

The Stories in this anthology are works of fiction. Names, characters, places and incidents are products of the authors' imaginations or are used factiously and are not to be construed as real. Any resemblance to actual events, locales, organizations, or persons, living or dead, is entirely coincidental.

Copyright © 2019 Short Stories of Forest and Fantasy

FIRST EDITION: 2019
978-0-9872863-9-0 (hbk)
978-0-9872863-7-6 (pbk)
978-0-9872863-5-2 (ebk)

The moral right of the author has been asserted.

Introduction © Charmaine Clancy 2019
Fantasy Map Illustrator © Martii Maclean
Paradigm Shift © Charmaine Clancy
Tinsel Fructify © Chris Radge
The Clockwork Prince © Martii Maclean
Blue Dog © Frank Prem
The Vala Tree © Georgina Ballantine
The Eighth Deadly Sin © Lea Scott
Forging Fate © LR Johnson
A Morning of Many © Maria Parenti-Baldey
The Cloudburst © Robert Walmsley-Evans
Joshua's End © Pamela Jeffs
A Tale of the Mountains © Rachel Nightingale
The Lost © Christine Kelly
Keeper of the Flame © June Perkins
Rainforest Sprites © Katrina Rutgers
Rainforest Healing © Renee Hills
The Six © Sarah Hegerty
Yowie on the Mountain © Paul Smith

No part of this book may be used or reproduced in any manner whatsoever without written permission, except in the case of brief quotations embodied in critical articles and reviews.
For information contact Info@RainforestWritingRetreat.com

Rainforest Writing Retreat is not responsible for websites (or their content) that are not owned by Rainforest Writing Retreat.

Cover and interior layout by the Self-Publishing Lab.

INTRODUCTION

Welcome to *Forest and Fantasy*, the second anthology in the OZ Tales Series highlighting the talent and skill of RWR Retreaters. This collective works of short stories and poetry will set you on an epic journey of adventure, magic and wonderment as you weave through high fantasy, urban paranormal and mystical myths.

While no boundaries were cast for the scribes, all authors were quested with the task of including 'Rainforest' into their tales. This seems fitting, as many of the following stories were imagined and developed while our writers were immersed in one of Australia's beautiful rainforests, Lamington National Park at O'Reilly's Rainforest Retreat.

Every year, a mix of established and emerging writers gather to attend the Rainforest Writing Retreat where they take part in masterclasses and on this occasion, our guests were inspired by fantasy masters, Isobelle Carmody, Marianne de Pierres and Trent Jamieson.

So brave adventurer, go forth and explore the forest, meet legendary beasts, pitch good against evil and unveil a mighty magic. But most of all, enjoy.

– Charmaine Clancy

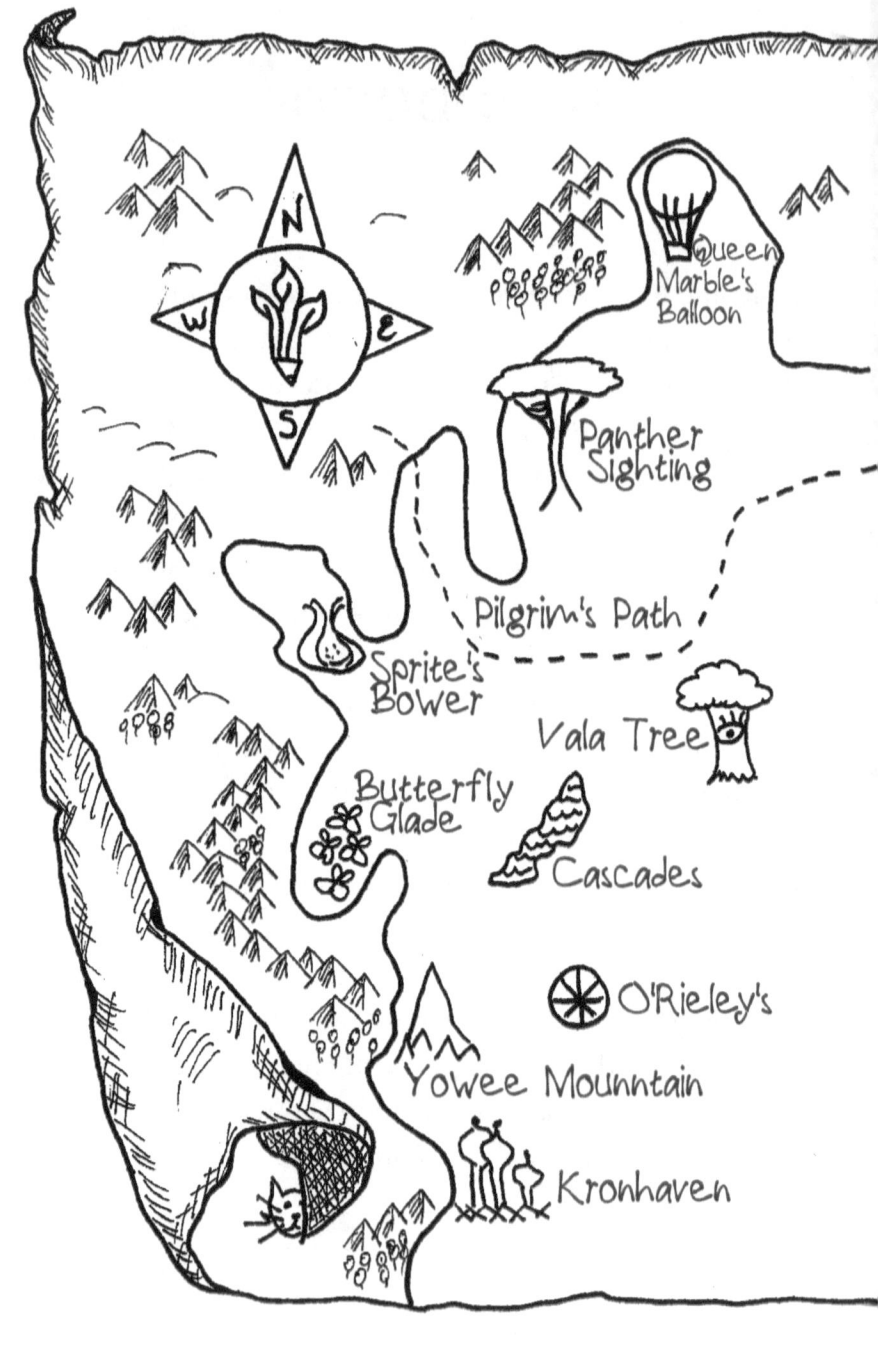

PARADIGM SHIFT

Charmaine Clancy

Mysterious *Panther Stalks Again!* I chuckled at the headline and dropped the *Sydney Morning Telegraph* onto my desk. Rumours of a panther living on the outer edges of the suburbs had been spreading like butter on toast. Some said it had escaped from an animal park, or a circus. Others believed we had always hosted big cats, but they were just really, really good at hiding. Usually. I mean, this guy had been spotted a few times lately. The stories were growing, like children's legends. *It stalks its prey at night. Didn't you hear about that little boy who got taken? My neighbour saw it on their morning walk and it looked right at her.* The truth? This was just a black domestic cat, albeit a little larger than usual. You want to see the real weird stuff? Just hang around the street below my office, Kings Cross, that's where the actual scary creatures roam.

At least you could get a decent coffee here. I mean, not here in my office, this poison was criminal. I cringed through another sip. One more client booked in and then I could go get myself a worthy cup of elixir down at the Piccolo.

I slid across the flip notebook Wendy had left on my desk. Wendy takes Tuesdays off so she can visit her mother. It simply said: *Mrs Jenkins 10.00 am.*

Great. Another angsty housewife. Still, consulting for the local law enforcement was fickle work and these housewives kept the lease on the office paid up. It's just hard not to get bored when you already know the answers.

The husband did it. The husband always did it. It doesn't even matter what 'it' is. *I think my husband is cheating on me.* Yes, he is. *Money has been taken from our joint account.* Probably, so he can afford that mistress. *My husband is missing.* Give you good odds that so is his secretary.

Yeah, it's all a bit cliché. You want something more original? Well, you and me both. I barely had to leave the office these days to close a case. My job is not what people think. Women don't hire a detective to find out if their husband is cheating. Nope. They already know. My job is getting the proof.

Of course, I couldn't just go and tell the client that. When a dame walks into my office, all teary and nervous, I have to pretend I don't have a clue what's up. I invite her to sit and offload what's on her mind. Honestly, it's all I can do not to yawn, but potential clients only want to part with two hundred bucks a day, plus expenses, if it looks hard. They're more satisfied if I end up presenting them with a long invoice.

I had a nice set-up, well, an okay set-up. All right, my office was a closet of asbestos and Formica. But I was pulling funds together and had my eye on a sweet rental in one of those heritage buildings just a short stroll from Circular Quay. Couple more jobs and that tall arched window and added reception area would be all mine.

So when her silhouette appeared at my office door, I did my best to prepare an expression of surprise and sympathy. *Oh, a lady here in my office? Whatever could be the problem?*

Only, the door opened, she stepped in and … wow.

It's easy to act sympathetic when they're pretty enough, but this dame? My heart was absolutely breaking for her. Her skin was shiny bronze. Her hair, the colour of liquorice, fell in waves right down past her waist, a bold change from the way girls were wearing their hair all short and curly this year. It was the eyes that got me, though. They were blacker than the subway in a power shortage and they had this curious curve-up at the edges. I could see myself sinking into them and I wanted to plunge into the rest of her.

'Thank you for seeing me, Detective Walker.' There was a deep accent to her voice, maybe Colombian.

'Please, call me Tom, Mrs Jenkins.' My voice purred in a way I usually reserve for prey at Freddy's Bar on a Friday night, and I waved invitingly to the chair opposite. 'How can I help?'

She pulled out the chair and sat, skipping the ritual. Most wives who come in here scrunch their noses up at the shabby upholstery, just to let me know they belong somewhere better. And yet, they all sit.

The silence was thick, but I'm patient. Comes with the job, I suppose.

She held out a little longer than the other wives, but eventually said, 'It's my husband.'

I could lap up that voice like milk.

'Go on, Mrs Jenkins.' I reached out a hand across the desk and covered hers, pretending it was for sympathy.

'I believe he's having an affair.'

Yawn.

She sits up straighter. 'I believe he's planning to kill me.'

Okay, not so boring.

I have a particular skill that makes detecting the perfect occupation for me. I go unnoticed and I'm easily forgotten. So, following Mr Jenkins around was a breeze. My steps were soundless on the pavement; he didn't even know I was only a few paces behind. Mr Jenkins had to be the dullest trace I'd ever had. For two days I stalked him to his office, and out to pick up his dry cleaning. I observed him order lunch and eat on his own.

I thought things would get interesting when I shadowed him to a residential house outside of town after work. No such luck. Turned out it was an exotic bird-club meeting. I also learned, from loitering in the lavender patch outside the homeowner's window, that Jenkins was in fact the president of the club.

At first I figured this must be a cover. Instead of birds, they'd actually be discussing territories for drugs, embezzling funds from the company they worked for, or, at the very least, be a group of older men discussing tactics for finding young girls. No, these guys were legit. They spent two hours discussing a range of species of parrots from the Colombian rainforests. There might have been something interesting in that, but I can't say for sure. I curled up in that garden bed and took a much-needed nap.

It wasn't until the third day that I caught Jenkins out.

Around two in the afternoon, I was considering calling it a day and taking up that job Bunty was offering. I could pull two service fees at once. I stretched, grabbed my belongings from my stash spot behind the second dumpster in the alley by Jenkins' office block, and stepped out onto the pavement.

That's when Jenkins emerged. I could have walked right past him—he had no idea who I was. But there was something about him that was different, that made me suspicious.

He was smiling.

So, I followed right behind, like I had every other time, but not invisibly this time. In my suit, with a camera flung around my neck, I was pretty obvious. Luckily for me, Jenkins had other things on his mind. He practically skipped down the street. I was sure I'd catch him with his mistress.

He walked three blocks and then paused, looked into a store window and opened the door. A pet shop? Great. Jenkins' big secret was probably a cockatoo.

Instead, he emerged a few minutes later holding hands with a short blonde. She was cute in a wholesome, not-skipping-any-meals kind of way, but I had to wonder why Jenkins would be snacking on this apple pie when he had a dish like Yvette at home.

Taking a few snaps of the happy couple, I kept on their tail right through town until they arrived at their destination: the registry office. It dawned on me then that Blondie was a little overdressed for a day's work in a pet store—a white linen suit with a matching fascinator. They were heading in to exchange vows. Greedy, Mr Jenkins, very greedy.

I snapped them entering the venue and headed around the corner to the nearest fast-development store.

A couple of hours later I had my Kodaks and was in a cab on my way to the Jenkins' residence. I figured Mrs

Jenkins—that is, the first Mrs Jenkins—and I would not get caught out. After all, Jenkins wasn't likely to bring his new bride home to the old one.

Sometimes dames get sobby when they find out the truth, while others get offended, as if it's my fault, and every now and then I get a scorned wife throw herself at me. Maybe it's revenge, or maybe they're finally allowing themselves to indulge. I don't usually bother asking why. I was hoping Yvette would turn out to be the latter. My hunger for her had been tearing at my insides. Plus, if she did get indignant, she looked like she'd have a mean right hook.

Yvette was not crying, not angry and not lustful. She was just ... not. I knew that as soon as I stepped inside, leaving the front door ajar.

Chairs lay on their sides, smashed plates littered the kitchen adjoining the living room, and a birdcage on the floor was empty, its door open. There'd been a fight in here. Judging by the splatters of blood on the floorboards, it wasn't the kind where you can kiss and make up after.

'Yvette?' I didn't expect an answer.

I followed the stains on the flooring to the bathroom. They led right up to the pink enamel tub. In the tub, it looked like someone had tried to make soup ... with Yvette. It was a bloody mess and caught in the drain catcher among handfuls of long, wavy black hair and a couple of blue feathers was a lump. An ear-shaped lump.

Damn it. When did Jenkins get the chance to off his wife? It must have been somewhere between nine pm last night, when I last spoke to Yvette on the phone, and seven-thirty am today, when I picked up Jenkins' trail into work.

But why didn't Jenkins finish cleaning up the scene? He'd obviously disposed of the body, so why not wipe away the blood and reset the furniture?

I walked back out to the living area, plucked the receiver off the Jenkins' phone and dialled the cops. While I gave my details to the officer on the other end of the line, a squawking caught my attention. I leaned to the side and looked out the sliding back door. In the top branches of a fig tree sat a huge blue parrot. Must have been Jenkins' rare Colombian rainforest bird that he'd been droning on about the night before at his little club.

I wondered briefly if Jenkins had been more passionate about his parrots than his wife. If she'd let the thing go out of jealousy and he'd just snapped. After all, he'd already been planning to replace her.

Something still bugged me, though. Was Jenkins going to run with the new bride? If so, why hide Yvette's body at all? Maybe Jenkins had a screw loose.

The police got all the info they needed from me and the neighbours, who all confirmed they'd seen Yvette many times since Jenkins had returned from his trip abroad three months before. They said there'd been a lot of yelling coming from the house over the last week or so. A few also admitted they'd never seen Jenkins and Yvette together.

She'd told a few neighbours that he didn't like her going out of the house, so she could only talk to them while he was at work.

Jenkins himself made it all too easy. The chump turned up at his house later that night with his new bride. Poor girl had no idea he'd already been hitched and that Jenkins was in fact completely loopy. He claimed he'd travelled home from Colombia alone and that Yvette had just 'kind of turned up'. He said it was 'all that damned bird's fault'.

The cops obviously dismissed his rants and took him off to jail, while a mortified young pet-shop assistant watched on.

Something hadn't quite gelled with me, though. And those feathers amongst the hair, those damned blue feathers. There was a piece missing in this puzzle and I couldn't let it go. I was going to have to investigate in a way very new to me: at the library.

On my way, I stopped by Madam Carlotta's. Carlotta has a little shop next to the Piccolo. Her shop-front title applies to the two businesses she runs. In one of them she is a mystic, reading palms and prescribing healing herbs; in the other she is as obvious as her girls.

Although it's unlike me to work a case for free, I found myself studying at the library each morning and returning to Jenkins' house each afternoon to try to catch that blue parrot. My newly obtained education now enabled me to label it a hyacinth macaw.

I stood in the Jenkins' backyard, holding out my palm, hoping the sugared bread would be a temptation. Each afternoon the bloody parrot would sit on a lower branch and just watch me.

That's okay. I'm nothing if not patient.

Back inside my one-bedroom apartment, which had an even danker outlook than my office, I brewed a late-night beverage and walked about to check that all the windows were shut and locked. It didn't take long; there are only three. I poured the elixir, a heady mix of coffee and cacao, into two slightly chipped mugs.

A soft tapping came at my door. The way someone knocks when they're not sure they want you to let them in.

Right on time.

I carried the mugs through to my living room, depositing one on the Formica two-seater table, and continued to the door with the other. I swung it open and leaned against the frame, holding out one cup of steaming brew.

'Yvette.'

She stood on the landing in a man's shirt and pants, her hair cropped short and jagged. A bandage was taped to the side of her face, presumably where her ear had been removed. Her eyes darted from me to the cup and back to me with a wide-eyed expression that could have been wonderment, or fear, or both. Whichever it was, I liked it.

Even in her dishevelled state, she aroused a primal hunger in me.

Yvette's hands wrapped around the mug and she stepped past me into my own little nest.

We sat at the table, sipping our chocolate-y coffee in silence. Our cups were almost empty before she spoke.

'How did you know?'

My smile was slow and Cheshire worthy. 'I didn't at first. I mean, I knew there was something, but I wasn't quite sure what until I saw the feathers in with the hair in the tub. Nice touch, by the way.' I tapped a finger against my right ear.

She pulled back in her seat now. I could see that I wouldn't get any more out of her until I gave up what I already knew. Cat and mouse. I could play that game.

'You're not the first changer I've met. After they arrested that chump of a husband of yours ... wait, you never actually married, did you?'

She kept her gaze straight and didn't answer. That was confirmation enough, she'd have been indignant if I was wrong.

'Did Jenkins even know what you were? Or did he meet the bird once the two of you got home?'

A slight turn-up of the corner of her mouth. So I was wrong.

'No, he didn't,' I said. 'He didn't even meet you until you got home. Jenkins brought a bird home. So your true form ... it's—'

'Avian. Yes, I am what you call a—'

'Hyacinth macaw.' Two could play the interrupting game.

She raised her dark arched brows. 'Impressive, Detective Walker.'

I waved the compliment away. 'I told you, call me Tom. So, you get back to Australia with Jenkins, he lets you out of your cage in the living room and voila! You take human form. Wow, he must've been bowled over.'

She leaned in until her lips were within reach of mine. 'He didn't complain.'

'Oh, I bet. Only he was already sweet on someone else. And when your'—I air quote for effect—'honeymoon was over, he wanted to return to his boring everyday world with Miss Pet Shop Girl.'

Her lip curled up into a snarl. 'I do not care about her.'

I held up a hand to let her know she should let me continue. 'No, but you needed Jenkins, needed him to marry you and make you a legitimate resident here. I'm guessing you were planning on becoming a widow early on anyway.'

She smiled, and one of her long fingers ran along the outside of my hand. It was all I could do to stop myself from pouncing on her right there and then.

'So, the whole murder scene, revenge? After all, Jenkins will probably hang.'

She pushed back her chair and stood up. She knew I was playing with her and she was getting tired of the game. 'No, I will come forward tomorrow. I'll say he beat me and I ran. I'll tell the police that I was scared, so I hid. When I tell them that we were legally married, they'll believe me.' She stepped around the table until she was leaning over me.

I shook my head. 'No good, sweetheart. Even if they do believe your marriage is legit, they'll still deport you because your husband will be incarcerated.'

She leaned down and whispered in my ear. 'Then I guess I'll need a new husband.'

I gulped and pointed at her shirt, ignoring her lips brushing against my earlobe. 'Clever. The clothes, I mean. The police might have noticed if anything from your wardrobe was missing, but they wouldn't have checked Jenkins' clothes.'

Her voice was deep and smooth and delicious. 'I do not need these.' She unbuttoned her shirt, slipped it off and let it fall to the floor. Yvette was an amazing-looking woman, especially for someone who was actually a parrot.

Her bare hands reached out and started on my own buttons. 'I knew. When I came into your office, I sensed you were like me. Am I right?' Her hand pressed against my chest.

Oh, to hell with it. I stood and knocked the chair over. I grabbed her and pulled her to me. Her bare skin pressed against my bare skin. We fell to the floor.

'You are an avian, too.' She breathed the words fast and heavily from beneath me.

I pushed myself up and stared into her black eyes. 'Not quite.'

She didn't question me again. She just moaned. Come to think of it, that might have been me. All I know is, I'd caught my prey and I was enjoying the spoils, and enjoying even more the thought of what was yet to come.

Afterward, she rose and paced about the apartment. There's not a lot of space for pacing, so she did small laps around the coffee table.

I sat up, feeling my own agitation beginning. 'Relax. You want to change.'

'I ... I ... no, it's not usually like this.' She stood and rubbed her temple near the bandage.

I rose to my feet, shaking my hands to the sides. I winced a little. I didn't want to hold off, but I wanted her to change first. 'You feel compelled to change. Don't fight it.'

She spun and marched to me. 'What did you do?'

It was the first time I'd heard actual panic in her voice. It excited me even more.

I grinned. 'It was the coffee, well, the cacao, to be precise. Did you know cacao is an enchant-able compound?'

I jogged on the spot to hold off the change.

She clenched her fists.

We must have looked ridiculous, both naked, both trying to resist the inevitable.

'Why?' She shook her head back and forth, but I could see she was losing the battle.

I stopped moving. 'Friend of mine, she fixed it. The elixir will force you to change. You won't be able to change out of your animal state until it wears off. Which, I'm guessing, will be plenty of time.' I felt my body submitting now. My blood pumped faster, my limbs elasticised.

Yvette dropped to her knees, moving through the same process. 'But you will change, too?' And those were the last words she uttered before her beautiful smooth body digressed into a vivid blue parrot.

'I'm … okay … with that.' And my mouth could not form the words anymore.

I licked my lips and stood on my wide, black paws. I gazed at her with golden eyes. Panther-like. Not an actual panther. Just a really large black cat.

TINSEL FRUCTIFY

Chris Radge

Christmas was supposed to be a time of cheer and snowman building, but not for the Niklas family, and not for a very long time. Janice wondered if it was the sheer inventiveness of the tinsel they painstakingly handcrafted from pure silver that kept the wolves away. The werewolves, that is.

Janice sat cross-legged on the plush carpet of the lounge-room floor without a scratch on her, staring at the single speck of ancient, dead blood on the shiny tinsel lying limp in her hands. Cindy let out a huge sigh behind her.

'Why do we use the same old tinsel every year? Sally has new rainbow-coloured tinsel on her tree and ours is boring old silver.' Cindy had flung her arms wide open to encompass the mono-coloured scene in front of her.

Janice knew her daughter usually loved draping the long silver tinsel that floated light as fairy wings onto pinky-length pine needles. 'The perfect length for draping tinsel,' she'd said every single year. But that still didn't change the fact that Cindy now looked bored with it.

Janice closed her eyes, took in a deep breath and let it out slowly. Cindy's sixteen, she told herself. She's still a baby. I can't expose her to this life already. Or can I? She drummed her fingers on her knee. The crackling and popping of the fire pulled her from her thoughts. She looked up into her daughter's young face and knew that it was time.

Peering through the thickly draped lounge-room windows, Janice studied the silent snowflakes that drifted aimlessly on the breeze before settling on the Canadian pines already laden with snow. She usually loved the snow, but right now she wished the family was far away from this mess and they wouldn't need to have this particular conversation. A vision of their last holiday in O'Reilly's Rainforest in Australia flashed through her mind. It was no good worrying about it. This conversation had to happen eventually and it may as well be now.

'Well?' Cindy said impatiently, dragging her fingers through her long dark fringe.

'All right, all right,' Janice said. 'Come.' She patted a spot on the carpet next to her, making her silver bangles clink. 'Sit and I will tell you about our special family tinsel.'

'Come on, Mum, I've heard this story a million times before. How is one more time going to change the fact that we still have this boring one-colour tinsel?' She stared at her mother with a sense of righteousness and power that only a teenager could have.

Janice sighed in defeat and watched her daughter toying with the silver pendant around her neck, which Cindy had worn since the day she was born. 'Just hear me out, kiddo. This will be the last time you need to hear this particular story, I promise.'

Cindy was still ticked about not getting a straight answer yet again, but she saw the defeated look on her mother's face and somehow knew that telling the story one more time was actually important. She slunk down and waited for her mum to begin her story.

'This tinsel is very special,' Janice said quickly.

Cindy rolled her eyes and parroted the next line in her mother's usual story. 'It's been in the Niklas family for many generations.'

'Just sit and mind your manners, young lady.'

Cindy was taken aback by her mother's unusual outburst. It was enough to stop her snarky remarks and she positioned herself better to listen to the story.

'Over four hundred years ago, some of our family members, often the young girls, would be taken by wolves around Christmas time.' Cindy's attention was now locked fully on her mother. 'There was no reason for it,' Janice continued. 'The month of December was an evil time for the little town of Nuremberg, where your great-great-grandfather Heinrick lived. He mined pure silver and loved to craft special things at Christmas time. Villagers would come from miles around to see what was for sale to adorn their homes.'

'What about the girls?' Cindy interjected.

'I'm getting to that, just listen,' Janice said, perturbed by Cindy's interjection. 'Heinrick found that if he cut the thin pure-silver sheets into six-inch strips and pulled them so each strip became even longer and fine, like spun sugar, he could create wonderful glittery Christmas decorations.' Janice watched her daughter unconsciously spinning the family ring she had always worn; an exact replica of the one Janice wore herself. 'This was the first time tinsel was invented, by the way,' she added.

This pricked Cindy's interest. 'Oh, cool, I can't wait to tell Sally that our family actually invented tinsel,' she said excitedly.

Now it was Janice's turn to roll her eyes. She smiled and continued her story. 'To our family, the tinsel was much more important than mere decoration. When they draped it over their Christmas tree, the attacks stopped. They would still hear the wolves howling at night but they never came in.'

'Why were the girls being attacked to start with?' Cindy asked, anticipation in her voice.

'There's something I need to tell you that won't make much sense.'

Cindy grimaced at her mother's dramatic words. 'Seriously, Mum, you're always so—'

'There was a big pack of black werewolves that lived ...'

Wait, did her mum just say *werewolves*? She's gotta be nuts, Cindy thought. 'Werewolves? Are you serious, Mum? You know how that sounds, right?'

'That's why I've waited this long to tell you. They—'

'Werewolves? Big dogs with chomping pointy teeth? You're talking about lycanthropes, right?'

'Yes, yes and yes.' Janice raised herself to her knees. 'The werewolves heard that our family healed quickly and that we all lived well into our hundreds, which is why they began by taking all family members, men, women and children. They devoured them in the belief that our blood would give them the exact same healing properties and longevity, but nothing changed for the werewolves.'

'So they took the girls to have children with,' Cindy guessed.

'Smart girl.'

'At least the girls weren't being killed like the others.'

'No, but the werewolves took the girls to breed with, giving them to the alpha males. The girl had to be bitten first so she could change and be able to birth the children. One good thing is that the girl then became known as the matriarch luna of each pack and would rule alongside the alpha male. The bite would create a permanent mark on her neck, and the alpha couple would be drawn to each other forever.'

Cindy thought for a moment. 'Mmm, so that's why no one in our family ever gets sick and paper cuts heal really quickly. But if the lycanthropes now possess our healing powers, why are they still after us?'

'That, my girl, is a very good question.' Janice was happy that Cindy was getting the importance of what she was trying to explain. 'There's only so much interbreeding they can do before the bloodline becomes depleted of its healing effects and birth defects become apparent.'

The wind howled outside, and Janice decided not to take the conversation any further. 'It's getting late, let's finish this conversation in the morning. We're safe tonight, as long as we don't answer any knocks on the door,' Janice said, even though she knew that could not happen.

Janice stood up and took a very old, large book from the family's extensive library. 'Write down all your questions for the morning. Here's our family genealogy album, it might just give you some answers,' she said, passing the book to Cindy. 'I'm going to make a cuppa and go to bed. Goodnight, kiddo.'

'Goodnight, Mum.' Cindy wrapped her arms around the heavy, dusty book. She started up the stairs to her bedroom, mentally flipping through her memory photos. She thought she knew all the books in their library, but she was sure she'd never laid eyes on this one before.

Getting distracted was one of Cindy's flaws, and she tripped on the last step. The book flew from her hands. She made a desperate lunge for it before it hit the floor, but only managed to grab a corner. The book fell open and a photo of her rose-scented great-aunt Carol fell out.

'Mum,' Cindy yelled, but there was no response. She heard the kettle whistling and realised her mother couldn't hear her. She shrugged. All good, she would ask her mum in the morning. She flipped the photo over, but there was nothing on the back. Cindy had seen her great-aunt a few days before. There's no way she's a werewolf, Cindy thought.

The smell of strong coffee and sizzling bacon sent Cindy's salivary glands into overload. Last night's blizzard had gone, leaving a canvas of white powdery snow.

Her mother reached for her hand and inspected the cut from the night before. 'I can't believe it's healed so well, it was almost deep enough for a stitch,' she said.

Although the cut had been pretty deep, Cindy was sure she would heal quickly because she always had.

She remembered last night vividly. She'd thought it would be interesting to test her healing abilities. She had sat in her bedroom closet, pulled out her father's scout pocketknife and hoped that what she was about to try would work. Holding out her index finger, she squinted her eyes and sliced quickly, before she chickened out. It was more like a paper cut than a serious wound, but it still hurt. She sucked at the metallic taste of blood that tickled her taste buds. Pulling her finger from her mouth, she saw the blood stop even before a drop hit the floor and the skin slowly began to knit itself back together.

A knock at the bedroom door had startled her and she jumped up, hitting her head on the clothes rail. She dropped the knife and automatically tried to catch it before it hit the closet floor. 'Oh, crap,' Cindy said, looking at her hand and knowing this second cut was a doozy.

'Are you in here, Cindy?' her mother called from the doorway.

'Yes, Mum,' Cindy growled through clenched teeth. 'I'm in the closet.'

'What, may I ask, are you doing in—' Janice stared at the bright red blood dripping from her daughter's hand. She made a quick side step, picked up a discarded towel, wrapped it around Cindy's hand and pressed firmly. 'What the hell are you trying to do in here, young lady?' Janice was almost yelling.

'Um, experimenting.'

'And why, pray tell, would you want to do that?'

'For starters, it wasn't supposed to be this deep.' Cindy looked down at the blood that was starting to soak through the towel and winced.

'Let's get you to the bathroom and clean this up,' Janice said, still applying pressure.

Cindy had followed her mother mechanically, her mind zeroing in on what she'd just done to herself.

'Cindy? Earth to Cindy.'

Cindy shook her head to clear it of last night's memories. 'Mmm?' she mumbled.

'What were you trying to accomplish with that little stunt?'

'I was just trying to see how fast we actually healed.' When Cindy showed her mother the first cut she was surprised to see that it was completely healed over. 'Geez, I knew I healed quickly, but not this quickly.'

'Well, now you know,' Janice said, 'so don't go trying anything like that again. Besides, the smell of blood will aggravate the werewolves outside.'

'Wait, what?'

'Yes,' Janice said, nodding towards the window. 'They're never far away this time of year.' She carefully unwrapped the bloody bandage from the deeper wound and saw that it had finally stopped bleeding. She wiped away the dried blood, leaving only a faint line that would soon fade. 'Now, do you have any more questions?'

'Seriously, is the pope Catholic?'

Her mother chuckled at the sound of her own favourite retort coming from her daughter's mouth, and Cindy grinned.

'So, how long does this last, these attacks from the, um … werewolves?' Cindy was still finding it hard to believe what her mother had told her. She had never seen any evidence of these so-called werewolves.

'Just during the month of December.'

Cindy sighed. 'That's doable,' she said, nodding.

'But that only pertains to our previous family, who are now members of the werewolf pack,' Janice said. 'There are still some rogue groups that hunt throughout the year, but mainly on a full moon when their powers are at their height.' Janice fidgeted; she had the feeling that the air around her had shifted.

There was a faint *tap-tap* of fingernails on the kitchen window above the sink. Startled, Cindy and Janice turned in unison to see a woman's face framed by the closed kitchen window with its country-style red-and-white gingham curtains, which added the only colour to the white kitchen.

Janice's sharp intake of breath told Cindy that this was not a neighbour coming to borrow a cup of sugar. A quick look at her mother's face confirmed that Janice knew exactly who it was and it was a meeting she was not looking forward to.

Wait. Cindy turned back to the window. Was that her great-aunt Carol? But it couldn't be. Her great-aunt was away on holiday right now. 'Mum, is that my—'

'No,' was the one-word answer Janice gave.

'Is … is it a …' Cindy stammered

'Yes.' Janice's eyes never left the woman's face. 'That was your great-aunt Carol's twin sister.'

'But she looks totally normal,' Cindy said, doubt creeping into her voice.

'I am, dear niece,' the woman said, stepping closer to the window and tapping the glass with a very long index finger. Judging by the expression on her face, the small gesture caused her searing pain. 'We have the same blood running through our veins.' She showed her wrists to the women inside the warm kitchen.

'That no longer makes us family, Rebecca,' Janice said, leaving off the 'aunt' from the usual respectful title. 'You are no longer welcome to speak to anyone in this house.'

'The child has a voice of her own and has to decide for herself,' Rebecca said. 'You know that, niece.'

'Don't ever call me that again,' Janice said vehemently. 'I am no longer your niece and never will be again. That ceased the day you decided to change into a stinking dog.'

A light knocking and tapping sound started in unison on all the external doors and windows. 'The pack is getting restless,' Rebecca said. 'Let's get to the point, and quickly.'

Cindy's heart hammered in her chest as her mind was drawn to the almost rhythmic tapping noise. She felt helpless, not having any answers, and grasped her mother's hand, hard.

'Be still, Cindy,' Janice said, 'you're safe. Each entrance and window is well protected in the old ways.'

Rebecca flicked her hand, as if dismissing the conversation going on between the women inside the house. But she knew this to be true. Neither she nor any other member of the pack could enter this home, surrounded as it was by salt bricks and lines of ancient silver embedded in every door and window frame. This was the reason that generation after generation of the family still lived in the grand old house.

'Cindy, as you're my great-niece,' Rebecca said, 'and I am the luna matriarch of this pack, I offer you safe passage and the rule of your own sister pack. Please join us,' she said soothingly, and ran her fingers through her fringe, showing her widow's peak.

Cindy's gasp told Rebecca that she had done exactly the wrong thing. She knew that her hairline was a perfect sign that she was a lycanthrope. Rebecca knew she had little chance of lulling this young virile female to her side now.

She looked hard into Rebecca's dark eyes, which were so different from her great-aunt Carol's blue ones. 'I renounce your offer forever,' Cindy said, 'and I stand beside my mother and our clan.' Cindy was proud of remembering that line from the family genealogy book she had read last night, describing how to renounce a werewolf's offer.

The anger of rejection seared through Rebecca. She forgot her own rule that stated no member of the pack should ever touch the house and thumped the window, rattling the glass in the colonial-style window. The howling of the pack grew louder.

Cindy and her mother stood their ground, not flinching, starting intently at the matriarch Rebecca. They both knew they had to wait this out. It was a testing of minds and nothing else. Rebecca could not harm them, not yet; it was still three days until December. Cindy knew it was unusual for the werewolves to try this now, especially since they were not at their most powerful. That was something else she had learned from reading about this exact situation in the old book.

'You will not win this battle, niece.' Rebecca drove her statement home hard, targeting Janice. 'Cindy will join us one day and the circle will be complete.'

Rebecca knew the line was desperate for replenishment; the werewolves were not healing quickly enough and dying too easily. The pathologist in her pack had been working on a solution for years with no success. Enlisting her niece was the only solution Rebecca could see for the near future, and she had her pack to protect.

In a last-ditch effort, Rebecca decided to use something she had not wanted to use. It was the way she had been lured into this life herself, without being given the chance to refuse; a life that she could not now, or ever, change.

The pull was faint but strong. Cindy felt an invisible tugging at the core of her being and started to shuffle towards the window.

Her mother's arm shot out to drag her daughter behind her in protection, but they all knew this motherly action was in vain. There was not very much on this earth that would stop a werewolf in its tracks, except ...

Her mother snatched up the open box of family tinsel on the kitchen bench and held it up defiantly. Her aunt recoiled into the shadows of the night. A howl of pain split the air. The tinsel was old silver, a hundred times more potent than anything they mined these days. Janice knew the immediate threat wasn't an all-out attack; it was cohesion. Not like vampires' cohesion, it was more complex than that.

That's exactly what the magnificent-looking grey wolf now standing next to his matriarch was hoping. He'd shown himself in his true form to impress the girl with his ability to turn on command rather than a full moon.

Cindy's mind was entangled with those of the young man in a wolf's body. Their eyes locked, and the transformation began. Their minds calmed and were filled with the picture of a dark-haired young man. She felt it. Actually felt his claws and fangs retracting as his human parts emerged. The pain was niggling, nothing like what she had read about. His fur retracted, tickling her all over, and she squirmed. It wasn't until the werewolf's snout started to change that she felt the pain of bone, muscle and tendon rearranging themselves; this was the real pain of a werewolf's plight. What had happened with the knife last night was nothing compared to this and it scared her?

She dropped her gaze. How could the werewolves endure this? How could they think she would want this life? She looked up to see the same young man she had seen in her mind moments earlier, except that he was stark naked. She swayed, and her mother steadied her.

'Not nice, Rebecca,' her mother said. 'You know this isn't allowed. We tolerate you with the understanding that you don't try that mind stuff with our family.' Rebecca's face was uncharacteristically blank.

Cindy's vision cleared and she saw the young man clothed in a wolf skin similar to his own. She couldn't form the words and just pointed at him.

Rebecca turned raging eyes on him and slapped him hard. 'Marcus!'

Indignation and rage crossed Marcus's face as he looked at his matriarch. Lifting his head higher, he flicked his long dark fringe, which hid his own widow's peak and the disfigured left eye and nose. He wanted Cindy for himself. Coercing her would secure him as a leader with his own pack. 'This is why we need you,' he said to Cindy, trying to appeal to her softer side. 'We need new blood or this will keep happening.'

'Are you ...'

'Rebecca's son, yes, and your second cousin.' Marcus lifted his hand, and the tapping and knocking sound ceased immediately.

'This ... you ... is not my fault,' Cindy stammered.

'No, but you can help replenish our line. Make us who we were once again.' Marcus was hoping he was making sense to this young girl. 'You probably didn't realise because you didn't know about us until today, but we have left your—our—family alone. It has been a very long time since we have sought replenishment of our line.'

Marcus was actually making sense to Cindy, but it didn't change the fact that, one, she was only sixteen and way too young to start thinking about having children, and two, she really didn't want to be a mythical creature. She was quite happy with her life, which, up until lately, had seemed pretty boring but it certainly wasn't boring now. Fancy me worrying about coloured tinsel, she thought absently. Crikey, wait till I tell Sally. Cindy was shaken from her thoughts when her mother spoke.

'That won't be happening, either,' her mother said her hand on her daughter's shoulder.

Wait, what? Did Mum just read my mind?

Janice did her one-head-nod thing again.

'So can I—' Cindy began.

'We'll talk about it later,' her mother said firmly to stop Cindy asking any other questions, for now at least.

Marcus knew he was losing Cindy. He turned slightly to his left, grasped something offered to him and held up a day-old naked baby. He watched the girl inside take a step forward.

The baby was missing an arm, but otherwise looked normal. Cindy was horrified. Had they done this to their own child? Were they barbarians?

'Can you imagine a wolf trying to run on three legs?' Marcus said. 'There's no way my son could one day rule this pack in my place.' He thrust the baby back into the arms of the female pack member who had handed it to him.

'That baby will be so cold out there,' Cindy said.

'Don't worry, Cindy,' her mother said, 'the wolves are warm-blooded and can withstand the cold weather easily.'

'Your mother is correct,' Marcus said. 'The child is in no danger from the cold, but he is in danger of being cast from this clan for being useless to us.'

'Mum, can we?'

'No.'

'But Mum ...'

Janice clasped her hands and rested them on her eyebrows. She rubbed at her forehead to relieve the tension. She knew what the impact would be of her next few words. 'Yes, we will take him and raise him as our own.' A shriek hit the air and Janice guessed it was the mother. 'He will be all right, young mother. He will be alive and will adapt to a normal life with humans, with this family but on one proviso, your pack or any other leave my daughter alone.'

'This is not accept—' Marcus began, but his mother took his arm and he fell silent.

Rebecca felt no love for the child, and nor could she see how he could be useful to the pack. Instead, the baby would only be a burden. 'Accepted,' she said. 'You can raise this child as your own.'

Rebecca was thinking far ahead to the time when her grandson would one day change and she would once again offer Cindy the chance to become part of the clan. She could wait and she had no intention adhering to the terms of her Niece's conditions. It would not be many years to wait for the result she wanted: a willing Niklas family member to join their pack and once again make it a force to be reckoned with.

Her daughter looked apprehensive, possibly realising the duty she now had to this baby.

Rebecca saw the look and understood that the opportunity was fading quickly. 'The babe will be left on your front doorstep in one hour. Take him, leave him, I don't care. Name him what you want, he's nothing to us now.'

Is this woman for real, Cindy thought. How could she be my family?

Rebecca howled in response and fled as quickly as she had come, leaving with all her clan.

The shoulders of both women relaxed as the tension inside them left.

'Well, that was terrifying,' Cindy stated matter of factually.

'I reckon you could say that. But now we have a whole new problem on our hands.'

'The baby,' Cindy said.

'Yes, the baby, what are we going to do with a young one in the house? You're going to have to help, a lot.'

'Sure.' She said nodding her head enthusiastically.

'Hey, I thought your aunt Carol was an only child,' Cindy said, changing the subject.

'No, she was a twin.' Janice's mind drifted off into memories. 'The family doesn't talk about Rebecca and her terrible decision except in rare situations.'

'Like now, hey.'

'Yep, like now, honey.' Janice said.

The child was left in a basket at the front door, swaddled in what looked suspiciously like wolf fur. The wind had picked up again, and almost drowned out the baby's cries.

The pack watched from the treeline, waiting to see if the two females inside would keep their bargain.

Hearing faint cries on the wind, Janice stepped outside, knowing she was protected by the sage, mistletoe and wolfsbane in the wreath hanging on the door; the salt bricks under the porch also ensured her safety. How unusual, she thought, gathering the baby to her warm body. He ceased crying and she looked down at him. We'll name him Lucas, she thought, and I will deal with that tomorrow. She kicked the basket and fur to the side.

She looked up, noticed the bush without a covering of snow and guessed the pack was watching. She turned and retreated into the warmth of her home. Janice had managed to buy some time for her daughter, but she knew the matriarch would not adhere to their deal. They would be back, when, she did not know, but for now they were safe. But apprehension crept into her bones. She'd felt Cindy's strong attraction to the pack, would her daughter be able to resist next time?

THE CLOCKWORK PRINCE

Martii Maclean

The Forest of Dancing Clouds was a deep and impenetrable place. Hidden within this dense steamy forest, behind a wild tangle of trees and vines, was the city of Kronhaven. From high points around the forest, outsiders watched and waited for the days when the clouds would drift away and reveal a glimpse of the city, with its towers reaching higher into the sky than any of the surrounding cities. At the very top of each tower were bulbous circular chambers ringed with sparkling leadlight windows. Each tower was roofed with a glistening golden dome that shone across the forest canopy.

The outsiders were awed by the amazing clockwork creatures that flew from tower to tower. They coveted the fortunes of this city, with its ability to manufacture anything a mind could conceive. Rumours spread throughout neighbouring provinces about the city's skilled alchemists and mechanists, and over time this envy had soured to hatred. Kronhaven faced constant attack and sought ways to defend the city's magic and technology.

Kronhaven's alchemists worked to strengthen the forest tangle. They called forth thorny briar and ironwood brambles, lacing each together into strong walls of hostile green vines and spikes, but now those defences were being breached. The attacks became fiercer and the losses more tragic with each passing campaign. The emperor guarded the city's magical knowledge ruthlessly. No one would take Kronhaven's secrets. He would protect them at all costs.

'These are troubling times, our laws must change for the good of the city,' declared the emperor. 'The mechanists will craft a soldier, strong and nimble, impenetrable behind his armoured metal skin. And the alchemists will set the fire of life in him. He will be a fierce-hearted clockwork prince, and he will fight and defend us, as any brave prince should do.'

Over the years, the mechanists and the alchemists had been manufacturing and breathing life spirit into all manner of creatures at the emperor's fickle whims, but they quaked with indignation at this unscrupulous decree.

'This is an outrage,' spluttered the alchemists and the mechanists.

Gaal, the master mechanist, stepped forward. 'We have made every lesser beast and bird,' he reasoned, 'but by your own ruling it is forbidden to build a thinking, loving automata.'

'That ruling no longer exists. My—our—need has never been greater,' the emperor justified. 'I will do whatever is necessary to keep our secrets, perhaps this creature may even bring about peace,' he huffed, glibly. 'It will be just another machine, like all the other machines you've made for me.' He glared down from his throne. 'You would do well to remember that the mechanists and the alchemists are in my service, and remember their place.'

The crowd backed away, leaving Gaal to face the emperor's displeasure alone.

The emperor stood and stepped forward, looming over Gaal. 'You will make me a clockwork warrior to defend us all, or you will be sent out to battle in its stead.'

'I will start at once,' said Gaal.

And so it was done. The rules had been the conscience of the city, and the safeguard for the creatures bought to life that had no choice in the matter, and now those rules were shattered. The clockwork warrior was fabricated; the alchemists drew the forces of life into his metal body.

Gaal watched as the ill-fated iron prince's eyelids flickered and clicked open. The clockwork man shuddered to life. He swayed as he sensed his body and its outer edges, wriggled fingers and toes. He lifted a hand slowly and lay it on his chest, and his face was joy and fear and wonder at once as he became fully and instantly aware of who and what he was.

Gaal stood back, fearful of what the iron man's actions might be. Was he monster or man?

The clockwork prince turned his head slowly this way and that, looking around the small stone room. When he saw Gaal, clicks and whirs rose from within him. 'My home?' he rasped.

'I suppose it is. What do you know?' Gaal asked the newly alive prince, wanting to know how much of a man he had made.

The clockwork prince seemed to ignore the question and stared around the lofty heights of the mechanist's chamber. Finally, the words whirred up from inside him. 'I know I am not like them.' He lifted a shiny hand and pointed to the glowing clockwork birds that sat trilling in the rafters. 'They are so beautiful ... I am for a different purpose.'

'This is true,' said Gaal. 'The alchemists have charged you with knowledge of your purpose. Your purpose will show itself to you soon. But you have only just woken, it will take some time.'

Gaal watched as the clockwork prince came fully to awareness that day. As Gaal had warned the emperor, the iron prince was far more than the birds and the lesser creatures that had been conjured before him. The iron warrior had been made like any other man, with a thinking mind and a loving heart, and with that thinking and love came reason and compassion, aspiration and desire.

When the iron prince learned his purpose, he went to the emperor and tried reasoning with him. 'I am metal. There will be no fairness in fight with the flesh-and-blood soldiers from the opposing cities.'

'Fairness has not bought us peace thus far,' blustered the emperor. 'That's why you have been bought to life.'

'I will not tire in the battle while my adversaries drop with fatigue around me. My iron fists will be rams against their soft flesh. My heart may be clockwork, but I still feel for their fate ... I cannot be your warrior.'

'You are made immortal like countless clockwork creatures, but I can order that you be unmade,' threatened the emperor.

The iron prince seethed with the ugliness of his existence. He thought of the sweet melodies made by the clockwork birds that perched and sang in every nook of the city. All the other automata bought some pleasure and beauty by existing. He was given one purpose—harm. Death. Gaal had made him with a mind and a heart. Though his organs clicked and whirred, he still thought and felt.

'If all my life will offer is cruelty and suffering, then unmake me now,' said the iron prince.

'Foolish metal man ... then you will be scrap iron left to rust.'

'Better to be unmade than to carry out the ugliness of your purpose for me. I desire—'

'You desire?' boomed the emperor, and he laughed. 'You are just a metal man. How can you have desires?'

'Metal or not, I am a person. I think and feel. I desire ...' The words whirred down into clicking thoughts. The clockwork prince trembled then spoke again. 'You want me to be your warrior. I will do this only if you agree to do something for me.' His heart gears flicked and fluttered, but he continued. 'I am unique and alone. I desire a companion, an automaton like myself, so I will not be alone in my immortality. As my reward for fighting your battles, I want a bride and a peaceful life.'

'Fight for us and we will build you a bride,' declared the emperor.

And so that great battle raged, and as the clockwork prince had predicted, the fleshed soldiers were no match for him, and the clashes were gruesome tableaus of valiant agony. Rank after rank ran to the battle. They fell and fell and fell. The clockwork warrior's iron hands cleaved muscles and broke bone. It took but a blow of his closed fist to wrench heads from shoulders. In the time between mortal heartbeats, he could reach in and pull the hearts out of the chests of the brave combatants. They would stare unbelieving at their still beating hearts, pulsing in his blood-tarnished hand.

Rip. Snap. Cleave. They fell. In the battle's lull, he would cradle those brave soldiers in his arms as the life faded from their eyes. He would lay them on the blood-soaked earth and his own heart would quake and shudder with the agony of what he had done.

He comforted his stuttering heart with thoughts of his bride and the immortal peace he would earn by agreeing to this brutality. Then he would stand and fight and kill over and again.

The lush green of the forest was splattered with red. Unrecognisable morsels of the brave fighters clung in sticky globs to the leaves and vines. The soldiers fought on, slipping in the puddles of liquefying entrails, tripping over the severed limbs, split skulls and oozing torsos of their fallen comrades.

'I am bringing so much pain to ease my own longing,' he whispered into the darkness.

The battle was finally won and the clockwork prince returned to Kronhaven. He heard murmurings in the streets, saying that his reward awaited him. He rushed to seek out Gaal in the mechanist's chambers, eager to see if the emperor had kept his promise. He surged through the doorway into the stone room and cast his war-weary eyes on his promised bride.

She was more beautiful than words could conjure. Her chassis glinted in the room's lamplight. The prince felt his heart click and whir. She had a smooth face and her eyes were closed, feathery lashes rested on her pearled cheeks.

The prince circled her slowly. 'Wings!'

His bride had glorious filigree wings fashioned from silver and bronze. The clockwork prince felt a gurgling effervescence deep inside him and knew he loved his new bride, immediately and so very deeply. He reached to touch her smooth face and saw his hands, red from the conflict. He looked down at his dull, pitted chassis, stained from the storm of battle blood.

'Beautiful, isn't she?' said Gaal, as he appeared in the circle of lamplight.

'Her beauty would take my breath, if I had any to take,' said the clockwork prince.

'It is the wings.' The mechanist rubbed his hands together gleefully. 'I made you, so I know your heart's desire. When you first came to life, the birds brought you such joy, so I knew these wings on your metal bride would lift your heart to love.'

'That they have.' The prince shuddered and looked down at his battle-uglied chassis.

'We will have you clean and tidy for the ball,' said Gaal. 'Meanwhile, my colleagues will work their alchemy and bring your bride to life.'

'Must I wait?' he pleaded.

'Just a little longer.' Gaal smiled at the pleasure he'd bought to the metal man's heart. 'The emperor wants to hear you pledge your life to the winged princess at the ball tonight.'

The ballroom was lit with a thousand lamps. High in the domed roof a thousand mechanical birds trilled and twittered, filling the room with their enchanting songs. The clockwork prince felt the gears in his heart shift and skip to keep time with the music. He swayed and smiled. Tonight he would dance with his winged love, pledge his troth and he would have a bride.

'When we are wed I will build us a cottage,' he murmured, and he swayed on, imagining dancing with his winged love. 'I will buy some of those birds and we can dance forever in each other's arms.'

The music rose and fell, and the couples twirled around the ballroom. The clockwork prince waited and wished that he could sigh, or perhaps shed tears of joy. He could do neither thing, but it mattered not for soon enough he would have his companion.

A gong sounded. The birds drew silent and the dancers ceased their twirling. 'Tonight we are here to celebrate our brave clockwork defender, and also celebrate a union that marks the beginning of a time of peace between our city and our fiercest former rival.' Everyone cheered. 'Tonight our brave clockwork prince will pledge himself to his winged princess and the time of peace will commence.'

The clockwork prince did not care about the emperor's declarations of truce. All he could think of was the beginning of his own hard-won peace. Cheers rose up again as the arched doors at the end of the ballroom swung wide.

Gears crunched inside the clockwork prince's heart as his winged princess stepped through the door, holding the arm of Gaal, the mechanist. Her face shone with pearl, as it had before, but with her eyes open her face seemed changed—she looked less like his peaceful bride.

He shrugged. 'I will see many aspects to my bride through our immortal life together,' he whispered to himself.

The mechanist also looked less joyful than he had before bringing the winged princess to life. The clockwork prince smiled and whispered again, 'Could the mechanist be sad to be giving up this beauty to me?'

She was such a beauty. The iron prince did not hesitate. He strode across to his bride, intending to sweep her into his arms and dance.

'No!' boomed the emperor's voice.

The mechanist shuddered. His eyes were wide.

The clockwork prince spun to look at the emperor.

'No,' the emperor said again. 'Before the celebration dance, we need to hear your troth. We need the pledge of the clockwork prince that he will marry this winged beauty that stands here before him now. We need to hear him declare that they will live together in peace at the beginning of this era of great peace for the Forest of Dancing Clouds.'

A great cheer rose up from the crowd, and up in the rafters the mechanical birds flustered, their metal wings tinkling as they settled.

The emperor beckoned the clockwork prince to the stage. The prince let go of his love and obeyed his emperor in this one last thing.

'Now, my brave soldier, say the words.' The emperor slapped the prince's metal shoulder firmly and pointed. 'Tell the winged beauty and all present that she will be your bride.'

The crowd parted, forming a path. The beauty walked with eager steps, her wings trembling as she did. The mechanist held her arm tightly, dawdling beside her as if to slow her progress.

'I pledge ...' Cogs somewhere inside the prince, near his mechanical heart, slipped and whirred, but he continued. 'I will make you my wife, and be true to you for as long as we shall ... exist.'

'You are all my witnesses,' crowed the emperor. 'The mechanical prince will marry this winged princess and we shall have our peace.'

A storm of cheers rose again.

The clockwork prince paid no head to the speechmaking. He thought only of his joyful new life, and his heart surged with happiness. He and his bride were both automatons, so their happiness could perchance last forever.

He ran down from the stage, through the parted crowd, and took his promised bride in his arms, holding her tightly. As the birds filled the room with music, he spun her across the dance floor. The prince stared into his winged beauty's eyes as they danced. Her face looked strained, and she winced. Her feathery lashes seemed wet, but he knew that mechanical maidens could not make tears, any more than he could have cried at the ugliness of battle, no matter how he ached to. I have so many new things to learn about my new bride, he thought, and he twirled her across the dance floor.

They danced on. Everyone cheered. He took his newly trothed bride's pearled hand and spun her, then drew her back into his embrace. Her wings trembled and tilted. He slowed their dancing and, holding her firmly, kissed her. He wondered at how her lips could feel warm. When he pulled away at the end of the kiss, he saw pain on her face. Now he wondered at why his hand upon her back felt warm, slippery. He lifted his hand and it came away red. How could his clockwork bride be bleeding?

He spun her in his arms. There was a ripping of fabric and she shrieked. The filigree, silver-bronze wings clattered to the floor.

'My darling!' The clockwork prince caught his swooning bride in his arms. He felt through the rips in her gown— underneath, flesh. Bleeding, wounded flesh. 'You are no automaton,' he cried. 'You are not my clockwork bride.'

The emperor's voice boomed again. 'She is flesh and blood, and not your princess, but she is indeed a princess. And you have pledged to marry her. All here tonight are witnesses to that pledge. This union will bring an end to the battles and peace to the Forest of Dancing Clouds.'

The clockwork prince stared down at the bloodstained filigree wings. The motor mechanisms were torn and twisted. He felt a grinding in the workings of his heart. He lifted the stained, twisted wreckage of his promised mechanical bride, squeezing the jagged metal, trying to pierce his hands so that his pain might find a way out of him.

'My true bride …' His words caught as his inner workings clenched and stuttered, almost ceasing with the effort to repel the agony of this unfolding truth.

'Was she ever really alive?' he asked Gaal, the mechanist. 'Was she really ever mine?'

The mechanist was pale and stricken. 'She was always yours and … she still lives,' he whispered urgently. 'She is tied to a tree, near the lake.'

The clockwork prince clutched his true bride's stolen wings to his heart and thundered through the crowd, dancers flying where they may, bones cracking. He ran from the ballroom and, pulling the doors closed behind him, crushed the locks, wishing he could crush the skull of the lying emperor, but all he wanted was to find his true bride. He turned and ran into the night.

Pounding through the steamy forest, the squawks and cries of night animals came from out of the darkness all around him. He found the trail that followed the slope down to the lake. Above the night noises he was sure he could hear singing. A sweet voice was singing. His bride, of course.

'Gaal gave my bride the gift of song as sweet as any bird's,' he said to himself. 'Music to soothe my soul after the torment of murderous battle.' He followed the sweet song and ran on. 'The emperor cheated me, but the mechanist had honoured the agreement by building me a bride that I could love forever.'

The clockwork prince found his bride, chained fast to a tree by the water's edge. He smashed his fist into the lock and pulled his bride into his arms. 'There is no one else but you for my heart,' he declared.

She shook her head. 'I stood frozen waiting to be awakened, and listened to the emperor's plan.' Sputtering rasps echoed from her mechanical heart. 'I know you have already promised yourself to the flesh princess, and a pledge is a pledge.'

'I pledged myself to you when you were no more than a desire in my heart.' He wrapped his arms around her, feeling the torn metal, her wings stolen for the imposter princess to wear.

'The emperor will find you and make you honour your promise to the flesh princess,' she said.

'We will go where they will not find us, where they will never think to look.'

The clockwork prince took his bride's hand and led her into the still water of the lake, stopping for only a moment to splash water and wash away their footsteps. They held each other close and walked into the moonlit depths of the lake, for they had no need for breath.

As the day dawned and dim shafts of light penetrated the deep water, the prince worked to reattach his bride's wings. He was no mechanist, he fixed the wings crooked and bent. Little water creatures could slip in and out of the mended edges, but his bride was whole and beautiful. They were free and they had love and music.

When the sun set, they walked up the silty slope of the lake and into the moonlight at the water's edge. The bride sang and they danced their wedding dance on the silty shore.

When the moon set, they washed away their footsteps and returned to the lake.

The days turned to weeks as the emperor, the palace guards and the false princess searched, but the metal prince and his winged bride were never found. Some swore there was mysterious music to be heard down at the lake at night. The emperor was cowardly and feared a curse, so he declared that no one could visit the lake after sunset.

Gaal, the master mechanist, burned his journals before another clockwork man could be made and subjugated. He was found dead in the alchemist's chambers with mercury on his lips and a note clutched in his hands: *Forgive me.*

Seasons came and went, and the clockwork man had many wonderful evenings dancing as his bride sang. He had his armoured skin, battle tough and sealed to protect his workings, but his bride had never been properly mended. The swimming creatures and the water were in her workings from the start.

As the years passed, she sang and they danced, but she gradually slowed, and one day her workings seized. They could no longer dance together on the shore.

But they could hold each other and be together, embracing on the silty lake floor. So he held her and listened to her sing until one night, as the shafts of moonlight shone gently into the depths of their watery home, his bride's bellows finally failed and her song stopped.

But they could still hold each other close and share each other's loving embrace. He held her and told her fantastical tales of faraway lands.

One dark evening, as he held her, she creaked and trembled in his arms. Her head sagged. He reached to cradle it, and as he did her arms crumbled away and sank to the floor of the lake. Her beautiful pearled body toppled. The clockwork prince crumpled next to her. He laid her pretty head gently on the soft dark silt. He stared at her closed eyes and her feathery lashes. He felt a searing pain inside himself and knew that, as his bride had shattered, his own heart would also break and unspool. Anger swelled in him. They should have had forever, but the brutal emperor had torn his bride's wings and robbed them of their forever.

The iron prince, stiff and wretched with grief, walked from the water on that moonless night. He staggered towards the city, vowing to rid the world of the emperor and his kind so that their cruelty would be gone forever.

BLUE DOG

Frank Prem

even in the day
he can see
the explosions

semaphore signals
sent
in lightning form
from a place
well beyond

at night
soundless
there is a flash
for every hit
and every death
out there

and
against his own desire
he feels compelled
to watch

can't turn away
from the drama
in the sky

he believes
now
that he can see
the dark of space
growing deeper

more and more
as each night passes
it seems
to grow

stars become
in absentia
as though eaten
by the day just passed
or
perhaps
it's only a trick
of battle

daytime
still brings light
shaded though
in hues of dull and brown
and grey

rain
has become
the falling down
of broken
space-fighting
stuff

and rivers
are dry
the forests broken
into brittle

whatever it's about
win it now
or not
every good thing
that ever was
has been lost

so come on
blue hound

let's slow-walk a while
through the spindle

among the char sticks
and rubble
might be something
you can eat

blue dog
poor boy
you've no strength left
for chasing

if something turns up

if
something
runs

I
will chase it
for you

I will try
the best I can
to feed you

THE VALA TREE

Georgina Ballantine

The leaf grazes Juni's cheek as it floats to the crystalline ground. He plucks it from the snow, tracing the leaf's serrated edge; the veins clear beneath the surface of ridged, yellowed keratin.

Juni wonders that the Vala tree demanded only fingernails from old Noké. The elderly baker was desperate, reckless, begging the tree to take any part of himself in exchange for his dying wife's recovery. Juni conveyed the tree's price: ten fingernails. Hardly a fair trade, but the tree's message was clear, and Juni knows not to judge.

Ten entire nails. Noké's screams still echo inside the tree's smooth hollow, though the old man left hours ago, wringing his bloodstained hands.

'Are you hungry?' Juni asks, out of habit. The Vala tree does not reply, but Juni knows the leaf he holds signals the Vala's contentment. It will not taste him today.

Setting the leaf at the tree's broad base, he leans the small of his back against the mounds of swollen roots. 'You will kill me one day, won't you?' he whispers, caressing the moss-covered undulations. He wonders, is he asking for confirmation, or satisfaction? The tree remains silent, but he feels the familiar dull throb of longing beneath his fingertips.

The first flakes of twilight snowfall dance beneath the forest canopy, brushing his bare skin. He shivers, wishing the tree would offer him warmth. He has not eaten today; Noké left no food. Victuals are not a requirement of invocation, but a kindness; one the supplicants should embrace more often, Juni feels.

A twig snaps in the distance. Juni knows the tread of human, despite the rainforest's dusk-time cacophony. Pleasure tingles within his chest, and curiosity, for few visit after sundown. The townsfolk's visits are dwindling as winter progresses. Juni imagines them huddling around their hearth fires; evenings of conviviality and bonding, when children laze on parents' knees and lovers twine on bearskins. This will not be his future.

Lovers. Perhaps the one whose feet now slide through snow and dead bark has come for such delight. The damp rainforest is a cold, unwelcoming place during the dark months. He cannot blame them for abandoning him, and yet he yearns for contact, though he is weak now. Too frail to satisfy, perhaps.

In summer, when the rainforest hummed with life, the people of the village came often to take their pleasure. Escape lay between their arms, a release from memory, from what the past had made him do. Both men and women sought him out, their awe reflected in widening eyes. They think him a person of import, the tree's mouthpiece. Dangerous, alluring, powerful, perhaps. Only the tree knows his suffering, for he keeps it concealed. Only the tree leaches his pain, drawn out through blood and will.

The approaching tread is light, likely woman or child. Perhaps Noké's wife comes bearing food in thanks for her rejuvenation. He shifts to sit upwind, but scenting the breeze, his mind recoils, his skin camouflaged amongst the twisted roots.

'Juni?' The voice is harsh, a deeper version of the one he knows.

Moving swiftly now through the stand of eucalyptus, the girl bursts into the clearing. She stops, scanning the tree's vast girth. 'Juni? Don't hide, brother. They told me you were here.'

The villagers have broken their promise of secrecy. Disappointment grips his chest, and fear, but he is not surprised; they would honour her claim of family, for the girl appears identical to him, soft-skinned, angular. Since the tree stalled the growth of whiskers on his cheeks and drained him of muscle, there is little to tell brother and sister apart.

She steps forward, the snow settling on her black hair in a fractal cobweb. As the moonlight settles on her face, his heart twists inside, wrenched by guilt and sorrow. A girl? No, a woman, and in so short a time. Her full cheeks are pinched now, her hips more rounded. How long has he been gone?

A blade glints in her hand, dark with sap. She has eaten recently. He scents the flavours on her skin: spiced lamb, sour pink plums, aged silverberry wine. His stomach groans; there is little point in hiding.

'Kika,' he says, testing the word as if doubting her name. Of late he has spoken little, and his voice cracks with effort.

Her head whips towards him, predator to prey. Has she come to claim her price? She cannot hurt him while the tree keeps him.

'Juni.'

A statement, not a greeting. Her shoulders drop as she moves forward, though he thinks she has not seen him yet. He sits up, feathers of white ice sliding off his torso.

Her eyes fix on him. 'You are naked.' She turns her head away, nose wrinkled in disgust. 'Here,' she says, flinging her shawl towards him, 'cover yourself.'

The woollen wrap falls, the knotted edge draping over his feet. Juni stares at the fabric. He does not recall the feel of clothes, and does not want to.

Kika glances back, blowing out a short, exasperated breath. 'I suppose I have seen everything there is to see,' she says bitterly. 'How you have not frozen to death, I do not know.'

She crouches to his left, her skirts brushing the tree's roots. He feels the tree shiver, scenting new blood, seeking out her suffering. And for the first time he knows fear as acid in his throat, and he pushes back against the tree's probing. *Not her*, he whispers inside, knowing he will be heard. *Never her.*

Kika shifts beside him. Despite her harsh tones, Juni senses she longs to touch him, for them to embrace as siblings do, but her hands remain in her lap. The silence grows between them.

'You are not pleased to see me,' she whispers. He does not respond, unsure of the truth. The twitter of bats alighting nearby startles her. Her right hand lifts towards him, fingers curving as if to grip his arm, but then drops back down.

'You have been away for two winters, Juni.' Her tone is softer now, familiar to him. 'I searched, when Father let me; questioned every traveller who came to town.' She studies his face. 'Last week, a woman came here from the village to seek Father's healing. The woman told us she had severed her own hand to give to a wishing tree in exchange for her children's recovery from blistering fever.' She leaned her face closer to his, tilting her head to look into his unfocused eyes. 'Once Father had bound her wound, she told of a man who lived in a forest beneath an ancient tree, a man who could be my twin. "Speaker of the Vala," she called you, and her voice shook with fear as she said the words. What does this title mean, brother?'

Beneath her curiosity, he hears the thread of jealousy. His lips part. At one corner of his mouth, the cracked skin splits, but the tree swallows the prick of pain.

'It means' — he pauses, swallowing — 'I cannot leave the tree.'

Kika hands him the flask that hangs at her waist, unscrewing the lid. While he drinks, she looks the tree up and down. 'It is certainly impressive, this tree. But not a prison, I think.' She sighs now, and he hears her loneliness. 'Come home, Juni. It is time.'

He returns the flask, and for the first time meets her gaze. 'Why would you want me?'

'You should come home. Things are ... different now. You belong with family.'

Family. Juni feels his heart begin to thump, memories threatening to seep back into his consciousness. He gropes for the nearest root, wisps of mist spreading through his mind as his skin connects.

With a sudden movement, she grips his face, turning it towards her. 'Are you scared to face what you did? Is that why you stay?' Her sharp nails dig into his cheek, but again, the tree takes his pain.

He shakes his head. The movement is slow, lethargic. Kika releases her grip. He recalls now her mercurial moods, from flicker to fire in a heartbeat.

'Mother is dead, Juni.'

The pain pierces his lungs, strong and swift, visceral. The Vala tree takes longer to respond. And yet, he knew. Not when, or how, but there had been days when the shadows felt lighter.

'Did you kill her?' His voice sounds controlled.

Kika laughs, abrupt and harsh. 'Me? No, she drowned herself below Fan Bridge. She was broken after you left. *Because* you left.'

The lines feel rehearsed. He sees Kika in his mind's eye, practising how she will make him pay with words, with weapons, with the memory of his betrayal. And he sees Mother, beside his bed, reaching ...

He breathes deeply. 'It does not matter, Kika. You must leave. It is not safe here.'

She jumps to her feet, spinning in the moonlight. 'As if I would leave now that I have found you again!'

Juni watches his sister, a crease of sadness across his brow. 'And Father? If you save me, will he love you more?'

Kika hesitates mid-spin, then completes the circle. She stops, facing him, eyes narrowed. 'I love you, Juni. You are my brother, my twin. That is why I am here.'

He knows she lies. He always knew when she hid the truth. Always.

She returns at daybreak, bringing sour bread and ewe's milk. Expecting thanks, she sets it before his prone form. Juni continues to stare at the sky.

'Eat, brother, you are skin and bone.'

'The tree is hungry.'

'Then feed it and leave.'

'I cannot leave the tree. Its sap flows through my veins, its wisdom through my bones.'

'Rubbish.' Kika screws up her face, incredulous. 'This tree only cares about itself. If it is true that it sprang from a wish demon's blood, then you are a fool to stay in thrall. It will kill you before midwinter's night.'

'The tree cares about truth, nothing more.'

Kika grunts in frustration, throwing up her hands. 'Truth? Does it know your truth, brother? What you did to me? For two years I have searched for you, and I find you a slave. You have not changed, Juni. Still running from your mistakes, still letting others control you, only now you put your faith in wood.' She kicks at the roots. 'I shall bring an axe and strike its pulp-soft heart.'

The tree's sinewed branches creak in the wind.

Kika's lips curl in disgust, but Juni recognises the fierce shine in her eyes; she is hoping to shame him into action. Now the shimmer spills over into tears, two swollen drops sliding over her cheeks. Her emotions swallow Juni in waves. He fights to slip back into the tree's oblivion, pressing his veins against the roots.

'Fear, Juni. The tree feeds on your fears, and on the fears of others who seek to change their path, their own truth. It gives back nothing but lies.'

Juni smiles. 'At the deepest point of fear, below the lies you tell yourself, is the only truth that matters. The tree keeps me safe.'

'Safe from whom? Father? Me? Facing your cowardice?'

'Safe from myself.'

She opens her mouth to retort, then closes it, her teeth snapping together. Shoulders raised, she turns and leaves the clearing.

A third time he hears her approach. No soft tread this time; he knows her stride, crushing twigs and damp leaves beneath her worn sandals.

'I asked in the village.' She marches through low ferns and spiky barkweed, arms swinging. 'They said this tree has flourished for a thousand lifetimes. It will survive without you, and what matter if it does not.'

As he raises his head, weary, she bends to grasp both his arms, yanking him to his feet. Blood rushes to his head. She tries to pull him towards her, but his legs cannot move. His face contorts, as if in agony.

'I cannot leave the tree.' He collapses back against the warm trunk.

'Stand up. Walk!' She slaps his face. He registers heat across his cheek, but the tree's call rings in his ears. He begins to shudder. She releases him and he crumples to the ground. 'You are dying, brother. Dying.'

Her fists clench and she reaches past him, digging her nails into the Vala's silky bark. 'What do you want from him?' she cries, dragging her fingers back and forth. Her nails scrape and split. She beats her fists against the trunk.

He sees her tears stream. Has she cried so since that last time, before Juni left? He remembers the sound of the bolt clicking home as Mother locked the door. Father's eyes, black with pleasure as he held her down, and Juni, sobbing when they forced him to hurt her. He cried every time. Every time. His eyes drift shut.

'He is mine!' Kika shrieks. 'I need him. His son needs him.'

His son. The words echo in Juni's head, binding together, scraping against his consciousness. 'We have ... a child?' he whispers.

Kika turns, the fire blazing in her eyes. 'He is a gift, Juni. A gentle boy, born of violence and regret. But I have raised him with love, kept him safe from Father's rage and Mother's impiety.'

Blood rushes through Juni's limbs. His mind cuts through the cloud; on one side, the throb of oblivion; on the other, a white-framed window, a straw-strewn room, and inside, a tow-headed boy. A child, sweet and earnest and alive with hope. It is hope that Juni has not felt for two winters, and it is hope that now forces him to his feet, wrenching him away from the tree's siren song.

Kika's eyes widen and she reaches forward to steady him. 'You will come?'

'Yes, I will come.' And the weight of memory, held at bay for so long, crashes down upon him. He sobs, 'I am sorry, Kika. I am sorry.' Letting the pain fill him, he lifts his head to the sun that now spreads orange flame over branch and leaf, sinking into the black ground.

Kika makes to step away, but sways, falling backwards. Her arms slide down the smooth trunk, her legs caving beneath her. 'My legs, I can't move them.' She writhes against the tree. 'Juni, help me!'

Juni throws himself forward, hands scrabbling against her shoulders, her arms. He tries to pull her up, but the tree's will knocks him back. He sees Kika struggling, growing weaker, her breath coming in short gasps.

'No! She is not yours to take,' he screams, lunging forward. 'She is not like me. She has no darkness.'

Kika grows limp at his feet, and he remembers as he tries to pull her up, remembers the first day he rested here with the world on his shoulders. The tree took him then as it now takes his sister.

'She is not yours,' he sobs, his strength spent, and he slumps down against Kika. Her face appears so peaceful, her breathing regular, but he knows. He shoves his hands behind her back, pushing to separate her back from the trunk.

And at last, the tree's will wraps him in darkness and takes its price.

The Vala leaf grazes Kika's cheek as it floats to the damp, black earth. She plucks it from the ground, listless, tracing the leaf's serrated edge. The veins stand clear beneath the surface of dried, red flesh.

Gently, she places the leaf on her lap, letting her mind wander, wondering why the image of a little boy drifts through her dreams.

THE EIGHTH DEADLY SIN

Lea Scott

Name, the form asks. *Audrey Walker,* I enter in my chicken-scrawl handwriting. I come from a long line of Walkers, both by name and by nature. *Occupation.* This one is a little harder. Pilgrim? Sin absolver? *Dog walker,* I scribble onto the blank line. It's more than a half-truth. The human race has always had its dogs—the immoral, the indolent, and the self-indulgent.

My ancestors walked the journey of the pilgrims, paid to carry the sins of others to the holy place, gaining them absolution for their vile and wicked behaviour. Most clients were undeserving of absolution, but the financial rewards have helped to build the Walker family dynasty. You'd be surprised what some people will pay for a get-out-of-jail-free card.

Not everyone in my family follows the 'Walker' tradition. You have to be born with the clairsentient gene, which means having the ability to take the feelings of others into your own body and carry them into the other realm. I've been a 'clear feeler' for as long as I can remember. There was never any question that I would join the family business, despite my impediment.

The rest of the questions on the form are straightforward. I finish with my illegible signature and wheel myself up to the reception desk. The registrar scans my form with a furrowed brow as if I am missing part of my brain, not my leg.

She looks down on me in my wheelchair with pursed lips. *'Dog walker?'*

If I could stand, I'd slap her. Instead, I ball up my anger and tuck it away in a safe place where I keep Wrath hidden. I've carried enough of that sin for other people to know how it can be your undoing.

I offer her my most enigmatic smile. 'I am resourceful,' I reply. 'My father always told me I could do anything if I put my mind to it.'

She rolls her eyes and looks back down at the form. 'Take a seat. The doctor will be with you shortly.'

Based on my long relationship with the medical profession, I know this is a line that is often touted but rarely true. I've come prepared. I push myself over to a well-lit spot by the window and pull out a file that contains profiles for potential new clients. I want to select my next client with care, because this one will be a big milestone for me. It can't just be any run-of-the-mill sin. It has to be one of the big and deadly Seven.

My skin tingles all the way up my arms to my fingertips as I open the file. It will be the first time I can actually travel the pilgrimage route on foot. I'm here today to have my first prosthetic leg fitted.

Kate Morgan is the first client in the folder. *Gluttony*, her sin summary reads. I inspect her photograph. Chubby faced with sad eyes. She's definitely out. Last time I took on a Gluttony client and carried her sin, I put on ten kilos and she ended up looking like a supermodel. Do you know how hard it is to lose ten kilos when you can't run? I toss the profile aside.

Willie Sharp, *Lust*. Hot bod with an uber-confident smile. These ones are often interesting, sometimes even fun. I feel my nether regions warming as I think about the last time I took on the emotions of a Lust client. Tempting, but I toss it aside, too. I want my milestone pilgrimage to be a little more momentous.

Margie Henson, *Envy*. I have too much of that already. *Toss*.

Tommy Burnett, *Pride*. Too old and boring. *Toss*.

Phyllis Merriweather, *Sloth*. I'm eager to achieve this in a hurry, not at a snail's pace. *Toss*.

None of them are grabbing my attention in the way I'd hoped.

I check the clock. I have been waiting for forty-five minutes. There is only one file left and I stare at it wide eyed.

Roscoe Carver, *Greed*. Now here is a creditable sin. Everyone knows that the desire for material wealth or gain is the root of all evil. Evil is what is written in his close-set beady eyes. Roscoe Carver has done some very bad things in the name of Greed, but he has terminal cancer and not long to gain his absolution. He seems a worthy sinner for my landmark journey. By the time I've finish reading his profile I am sure he is the one.

'Ms Walker,' the doctor calls.

I am resourceful. The motivation to take on the sins of Roscoe Carver gets me through the pain of the fitting, and the ongoing physiotherapy for the next few weeks. I was born for this job, and if it weren't for an unfortunate childhood accident I would be as far advanced in my career as my younger brother. I shut Envy back inside with all the other emotions I have gathered from sinners and have worked so hard to lock away. It is catch-up time.

With my mind fully focused on Roscoe Carver, within a few short weeks I am able to walk alone. As my father has always said, I can do anything if I put my mind to it.

I lower myself onto the mattress, shoulders slumped. I'd honestly thought I would deliver Roscoe Carver's sins today. My new leg has slowed me down much more than I'd anticipated. I'd overheard my father talking about a portal to the other realm located in the rainforest in

Lamington National Park. I was sure I could find it on my own. I wanted to prove myself to all of them.

A couple of times I thought I was close, but I used up my energy racing toward flickering lights that turned out to be nothing more than insects buzzing in the filtered rays of sunshine that broke through the rainforest canopy in long streaks. It was stupid not to ask for directions. After trekking through the rainforest all day, I've had to admit defeat and now I'm holed up in an expensive rainforest retreat for the night, licking my wounds in front of a crackling fire.

Bang! There it is again. Were those pesky revellers staying next door back from the bar? I am halfway off the bed to tell them off when the door handle rattles. There is a crash, followed by the sound of splintering timber. Someone is trying to break through the door.

I open my mouth to cry out, but my voice catches in my throat. I might alert the intruder that I am right here on the other side of the door. If I'm quiet, he might just leave. I press my hands together, but it is wishful thinking.

There is a shout from outside the door and my breath quickens. I have to get out of the room before he makes it in. My legs launch me from the bed and lunge me toward the bathroom. The door crashes open behind me. I press myself up against the wall on the other side of the doorway then spin my head around, searching the shadowy room for a weapon. I can't see anything helpful. I am on my own against the intruder.

I edge along the dim wall, trying to make it to the small window. Maybe I can escape through it. I am almost out when I feel a hard tug on my leg. I am dragged back into the room. A large figure looms over me.

'Hand it over!'

'Hand what over?' I ask, shrinking away from him. 'I don't know what you're talking about.'

His mouth twists into a cruel snarl, highlighting the long scar that extends from his lip to his chin. 'Don't give me that Little Miss Innocent bullshit. I overheard Roscoe askin' you to carry his sins to the holy place. I'm not stupid. I know just what he was talkin' about. Where's the cash?'

If he weren't so menacing, I would laugh at his stupidity. 'There is no cash. He meant his sins, literally. He was looking to make up for all the bad things he's done. He's sorry for the life he's lived. He wants absolution.'

'Huh. Roscoe sorry?' His spittle sprays across my face. 'You've got to be kidding me. Roscoe doesn't care about anyone but himself. Greedy bastard never has. Been shipping drugs into the country for years, kids dying all over the place. It's only ever been about Roscoe and his hip pocket.'

Another mistake. If I'd asked Roscoe to pay in advance I could have just handed over the cash to get rid of this brute. I implore him with my eyes. 'You're right. It was. But all that changed when he found out he was dying.'

'Enough. He owes me. Tell me where the cash is, *now.*' He pulls a gun from beneath his shirt and aims it at my head.

I duck and try to dive into the bathroom, but I feel a terrifying yank that dislocates my prosthetic leg from my knee. A searing pain erupts in my ears as a shot rings out and the bullet buzzes past my cheek. My vision blurs. All the Wrath that I had tucked away in that safe place comes tumbling out, along with all the other sins I have gathered and repressed during my career. My hands develop a mind of their own, grabbing for the prosthetic limb and striking out with a fury I didn't know I possessed. Judging by the thudding sounds, I am sure it is making contact with soft flesh. Another shot rings out and the bullet grazes my temple. I feel myself sinking to the floor.

I come to with the sensation that I am being chased, and I push against empty air. I notice the man sprawled just a few metres away, a pool of blood radiating from his head. I attempt to stand, but lurch sideways. Glancing across the room, I spot my new leg. It lays prostrate on the floor, halfway between the man and me. I shimmy over to his side and stare into his glassy eyes. I can tell he is dead by the way they gaze lifelessly at the ceiling, but I feel for a pulse, the way they do in the movies. Nothing.

There is a loud knock on the door. 'This is the police. Open the door.'

Holy moly, how am I going to explain this?

After a short pause, the voice repeats, 'This is the police. There has been a report of gunshots from this room. Is anybody there?'

I find my voice. 'Yes, yes. I'm coming,' I call out, as I scramble toward my prosthetic leg. I roll up my trouser leg and then strap it in place, ensuring I have fully covered it before racing to the door.

The weeks of painful physiotherapy I've endured have paid off. I lead the uniformed police constables into the living room with a smooth stride. I sense their shock when they look down at the dead man.

'I was just about to call you,' I say in a strained voice.

'My God, what happened here?' the younger of the constables asks.

'I don't really know. I went out to get some food, and when I got back there were two men in my room.' I pause to take ragged breaths. 'They were shouting at each other and one had a gun.'

'It's okay, just take it slow.'

'I turned and ran. I heard him crash through the door behind me. All I remember is seeing this hand coming toward me. He must have knocked me out. I'm so sorry I can't tell you anything more.' I look across at the body and shudder. 'I guess he must have done that, too.'

The older and more experienced-looking constable takes over. He pulls out a notepad. 'Senior Constable Henries, ma'am, can you tell me your name and your business in town?'

'Yes, my name is Audrey Walker and I'm on my way north for work. I had just stopped off here in this motel for the night. I don't know anybody here and I don't know this man.'

Henries starts jotting down my recollection of events. 'Unfortunately we didn't get much information from the triple-zero call. Can you give me a description of the other man?'

'I didn't actually see him.' I put my hands over my face. 'It was dark. All I remember is seeing his hand. I ... I closed my eyes, I was so frightened,' I say through my trembling hands. Now that I have let loose the bottled-up sins of my clients, I can feel Pride wanting to take credit for my performance. I resist the urge to puff out my chest.

'You didn't see anything? Not the colour of his hair, his height, anything he was wearing that might help identify him?'

I feel my eyes moisten and allow myself to give in to the emotion. I look up with liquid eyes and shake my head. 'Sorry. Nothing.'

He tempers his voice. 'Okay, well, we'll get the crime-scene boys over here and see what they can turn up. He might have left his grubby prints behind. Bit of luck, we'll have them on record.' He motions to the younger constable to move away to make the call. 'And don't touch anything,' he warns.

Henries reaches out to take my quivering hand in both of his. 'I think we should move outside.' He points to the body. 'You don't want to be forced to look at that any longer.'

I struggle to move. Sloth seems to have overcome me. As I pass a wall mirror, I notice my eye is turning purple. Damn it. I'm going to have to go to the trouble of covering it with a thick concealer for ages. A crimson split in my lip glistens in the light. I curse under my breath. That will be harder to hide. I will just have to avoid my mother until it heals. She never wanted me to go into the family business, and this will only give her another reason to harp on at my father about it.

'Ms Walker?' The constable nudges my elbow and I realise he has been talking to me.

'Oh, sorry, what did you say? I was miles away.'

'Hmm, understandable. I just asked if you knew of anyone who might have followed you here, or who might want to harm you in any way?'

Another face appears in the doorway and my eyes narrow at the irony. If ever I had made an enemy without cause, then here he was, and a multi-generational enemy at that. Senior Detective Mark Riley had never made it a secret that he disliked the Walker family, nor had his father, or his father before him. They had always suspected us of criminal activity because they had never been able to work out how we had amassed our fortune. We cover our tracks well with a number of legitimate businesses, operated, of course, by the non-clairsentient members of the family.

What the hell is Riley doing here? Has he been following me?

Senior Constable Henries is awaiting my answer with unexpected patience. He clears his throat in an attempt to regain my attention.

I stand tall and glare at Riley as I answer Henries. 'No. I don't think I, or any of my family members, for that matter, have done *anything* to make enemies.'

From the doorway, Riley speaks with unnecessary brusqueness. 'I'll take over from here.' He presses his way into the room, flashes his badge and motions for Henries to leave the room.

'Yes, Detective Riley,' Henries says, looking like a child eager to please his parent. 'Would you like me to run through my notes with you?'

'No.' Riley's tone is firm. 'That will be all.'

I flush then part my lips as I take in Riley properly. He is a very attractive man, with broad shoulders and strong arms that I suddenly long to slip into. Ugh! I recognise that Lust has reared its ugly head.

My jaw tightens and I fortify myself to stand up to the bully I know he is. It surprises me when Riley's demeanour softens.

He stares at the body, and then at me, with his steely blue eyes. His lips curl into a sad smile. 'It must've been hard for you to watch that man die right in front of you.'

I knew it. He is gunning for me and my family, and wants to take us down. I feel my hands begin to shake and move them out of sight behind my back. Fighting to keep my voice steady, I say, 'I thank God I didn't see it, Detective Riley. The other man must've knocked me out first.'

Riley sneers. 'The other man. Yes, tell me about this other man. Was he big? Small? Young? Old?'

I cross my arms. 'As I told the constable, I didn't see him.'

'You didn't see him?' Riley's pitch elevates as he speaks. 'A man is close enough to whack you so hard he knocked you unconscious and you didn't even see him?'

'It was dark. My eyes were closed.' How could I ever have thought Riley was attractive? My voice takes on an edge of sarcasm. 'We're not all as big and strong as you, Detective. I was cowering like a baby, and I'm not ashamed to admit I was bloody terrified.' I rub my eye and can feel the socket swelling.

Riley holds me in a long unblinking stare. 'Time will tell.'

'Tell what?'

'Whether you, or any of the Walkers, played a part in this crime.'

Wrath returns and I square my shoulders. 'What reason could I possibly have for wanting a man I've never seen in my life dead?' I scream at him.

'Interesting,' is all he replies as he turns and makes his way toward the body, gesturing for me to leave the room.

I wonder why he has dismissed me so easily. Is it what I have said? Or what I have not said? My thoughts churn. Was he going to try to pin this on me? My family had spent centuries keeping their business a secret and avoiding publicity. My mother will never forgive me if I've muddied the family name.

Men in overalls and white gloves pass me as I exit the room. 'What are they looking for?' I ask the younger constable.

'Anything that might give us a lead to whoever did this,' he replied. 'But mostly they're hoping to find the murder weapon.' He sounds a little too zealous to me, like he's still wet behind the ears. 'You know, in most home-invasion cases like this, murder is not the intent. The culprit could have ditched the murder weapon in his haste to get away. Or at least we hope so.'

I can't help myself as Pride takes hold. In a smug tone, I chortle, 'So you think that whatever he was killed with might be right here under our noses?'

'We hope so. He might have brought a weapon with him, or he might have just grabbed something at hand.'

I stifle a sly grin.

'We'll need you to make a list of anything of yours that's missing, once you're up to it.'

I start to shake my head to indicate that I don't think anything is missing when a spinning sensation starts in my head. It swirls down my body. My vision blurs and I reach out for the constable. He puts his arms under mine to steady me.

'I think I better drive you into the hospital, Ms Walker. You've got a nasty bump there on your head.' He looks down at my trousers. 'And it looks like your leg's been bleeding, too.' I try to protest, but he holds up his hand. 'I'm not taking no for an answer.'

'Okay, Constable, but just let me grab a few things.' I shield my bag with my body and fill it with what I need.

He leads me out to the car and opens the door for me. 'Just call me Jimmy.'

I try to wave Jimmy off at the door of the emergency department, but he insists on walking me to the registration desk and giving them the details of the incident. Once I am registered and seated in the waiting room, I say, 'I'll be okay from here, Jimmy. I'll call a taxi to pick me up later.'

'It's all right, Ms Walker. I'll wait outside. I'm sorry, but I have to take you back to the station after to answer some more questions.'

Once he is out of sight, I twist my head around, looking for a sign to the ladies' room. I allow myself to limp until I'm inside and then lock myself in a cubicle. I had strapped on the prosthetic leg in such a hurry that I hadn't taken the time to ensure the cushioning was in place around my knee joint. My stump now aches. I unstrap the burdensome appendage then turn it slowly to inspect the damage. I take some antiseptic wipes from my bag and begin to clean the blood off the hard plastic casing: the dead man's blood.

I hold the leg up to the light. There is a small dent in the shin, but it will be hardly noticeable to anyone who is not as intimately acquainted with the limb as I am. The dent it made in the side of that unsavoury man's head, now *that* is a whole different story.

I suppose I could have cried self-defence to the police, but what if they had connected the man to Roscoe Carver, who is no doubt well known to them? Riley might have pursued me even harder. Where would that have left my family if the police started to investigate them? I have to admit that I enjoy the perks of being a Walker, so I guess Greed played a part in my decision as well. I'll have to take care to regulate that.

Slipping a new pair of trousers from my bag, I change into them and throw the bloody pair into the sanitary bin. Nobody will find them there, and even if they did they would assume it was a menstrual accident.

I make my way back to the waiting room, happy for the long delay before I can see a doctor. It gives me a chance to work on my story before I have to face more questions from the police.

By the time I am standing outside the hospital, waiting for Jimmy to bring the car around, I am no longer concerned about Riley's threats. Without a murder weapon, I know that, unlike me, he doesn't have a leg to stand on.

Shifting my weight onto my prosthetic leg, I turn my smile inward. My father always told me I could do anything if I put my mind to it—even more, it seems, when I unite with the minds of others. That's my eighth deadly sin. I'll have to work hard to keep those emotions in check, but I'm sure I can work them to my advantage to fast-track my career. After all, I *am* resourceful.

FORGING FATE

LR Johnson

The swiping claw barely missed Ravaque's eye. His companion, Belenus, jerking him backwards is all that saved him.

The bear reared once more, mouth wide, roaring, but in that second a massive scaled talon reached out of the smoke cloud and snatched the bear off its feet, lifting it into the smoke and away from the two remaining armoured men on the mountainside. Small reprieve, yet there was still a distant cacophony of violence upon the wind.

War raged about Mount Olimbos.

Elves, dryads, mages, fae and other non-Havilah beings had formed the Confederation of Free Races and turned against the Havilah, the race of gods. Some of the gods had themselves defected, defiling themselves with their allegiance to these lesser races. Weeks ago they had taken Isiridil, the city at the foot of the mountain and the centre for the administration of Havilah rule, and laid siege to Olimbos, the capital city.

The war had been long, and while the lesser races were inferior individually, they had far superior numbers.

Surrounding the two cities were clouds of dust and smoke, lit from within by explosions, and lightning of all hues. Percussive explosions made windows rattle, the impact felt underfoot. The confederation had proven to be a far more formidable foe than any Havilah had expected.

By the end of this day, the confederation would win.

Ravaque, god of war and highest in command, foresaw the imminent defeat of the Havilah forces, and with his second in command, Belenus, god of forging, took a small detachment of soldiers on a covert mission to guarantee victory. Ravaque had sacrificed Havilah lives to slip through the confederation's weakest position and down the mountain to Isiridil.

'The command is wiped out,' Belenus panted, as he jogged toward the sprawling stone city below. 'Only you and I remain.'

'You are all I need,' Ravaque muttered.

'Are they going for the Seat of Heaven?' Belenus asked.

Ravaque nodded. 'They go for our heart,' he said. 'They will attempt to destroy it.'

They ducked into a ruined stable and watched as a troop of elves jogged past before peeling off and shapeshifting into the flittering forms of birds and soaring away.

'Can the seat be destroyed?' Belenus pressed, dark brow furrowed in concern. A trickle of blood ran down his thigh, and he discovered a gash in the armour at his side. Tearing off a portion of his cloak, he packed the wound and resecured his breastplate.

'Of course not.' Ravaque peered through a crack in the stable wall, and gestured toward the city wall. After checking for patrols, the two darted out of the stable and over to the wall.

Their armour was padded for silence. Ravaque laced his fingers over his knee, and Belenus hoisted himself up on top of the wall. With a gasp of pain, he pulled Ravaque after him, and the two slipped down the other side and into the ancient city.

Free Race patrols roved throughout the radiating grid of cobblestone streets, but they were light in the poorer sections of the city. It was through these that Belenus and Ravaque crept towards their destination: the Vault of the Host.

Beneath their concealing cloaks, both were decked out in their finest armour, as pride and dignity demanded: Belenus in silver and blue, and Ravaque in gold and red. Their wide shoulders and overlapping plates were an impressive sight, impressive enough to give even the boldest opponents pause.

Ravaque scowled. 'As war leader, I should walk Isiridil's avenues with an entourage of fifty warriors, not creep through the shadows.'

His companion nodded. 'I know. I did not expect so many losses during the diversion.'

'It matters not.' Ravaque waved the concern away. 'I have you, and we have been together on many campaigns. I trust you like a brother.' He gave Belenus a warm smile, which was returned.

'You have no idea how much that pleases me, my lord,' the silver-armoured man said softly.

They skipped a street to avoid a patrol of mages and fae. Belenus had his sword at his hip, one hand on the scabbard to keep it still. One mage might not be a problem, but two or more would draw too much attention, even for two gods.

Overhead, violet lightning branched across the smoky sky, followed by rolling thunder.

They needed to move quickly yet carefully. Elves were shapeshifters, and so every bird or stray dog they saw was incinerated with a silent blast of energy. They pressed their backs to a stone wall, listening for trouble in the street.

'Once more block to the vault,' Ravaque informed Belenus.

Belenus nodded and peered around the corner. Swore under his breath.

A squad of four ex-slaves lounged across their most expedient route, mere dryads by the look of them, their throats bearing the tan lines of their missing slave collars.

Ravaque's expression sharpened. He had a penchant for taking his time when ending a life, but Belenus rested his silver gauntlet on Ravaque's bracer to stay him. Their eyes met for an instant. Both sets of irises shadowed with dark intent, changed hue constantly.

Belenus' gauntlet tightened on the hilt of his sword. He slipped Ashril, the diamond blade, from its sheath and it glittered in the dawn light. Striding into the middle of the street, Belenus held Ashril aloft. The Free Race soldiers panicked and scattered, but before they could take ten steps each was reduced to a scattering drift of ash.

With merely a thought, Belenus had eradicated them all.

'Good work,' Ravaque commented heartily from behind Belenus. 'Once we summon the Host, all such disobedient ones will be the same.' He kicked a pile of ash.

'The status quo will be corrected.' Belenus agreed firmly, sheathing Ashril. He hid the shaking of his hand by gripping the hilt.

The god of forging had never before felt that killing was murder. He had crafted weapons of war, and had taken slaves' lives without a thought. Never had his hands felt bloodied the way they did now. Slaves were commodities, not people. That was how he had always lived, how his people had stayed in power. He had to remind himself of this and take firm control of himself as he and Ravaque ventured toward their goal.

The large stone edifice towering overhead was lined with sculptures of creatures of myth and magic, all snarling at those below. The Host. An unstoppable, vengeful army that would wipe out all dissenters once summoned. More than two-thirds of sentient life on the planet would die.

Belenus could hear echoing booms, scintillant energies dancing at the edge of perception. He paused to look up just as the wind changed. He saw the titanic forms of beasts of myth casting shadows across the twin cities. Dragons shot beams of energy from open maws and phoenix obliterated ranks of soldiers with a sweep of fiery wings. This was the true power of the Havilah. The ability to shapeshift, to change their form into one capable of harnessing tremendous energies.

The sacrifice was necessary to secure the future. Ravaque must reach the tower in the Vault, to summon the Host.

Ravaque was now several hundred metres ahead, and Belenus hurried to catch up. He was weakening, and one boot was squelching with blood.

The Vault of the Host was guarded by several groups of confederate soldiers. Elves, dryads and a mage guarded something they did not understand the purpose of, yet recognised as significant.

Ravaque growled in anticipation of the slaughter, his fingernails lengthening into claws.

But Belenus stepped past him. 'Allow me to serve.'

Once again Ashril rose, and even as the mage attempted to call power to protect himself his living flesh was reduced to ash. The elf next to him was frozen solid, lifeless. The guards were obliterated in seconds. Some were ash, some stone, and some frozen.

The god of war whistled. 'I had wondered where your loyalties lay since your daughter's disgusting act, but now I see your true feelings.'

Belenus spit onto the cobblestones in obvious distaste. 'Marrying a human was disgusting enough,' he agreed. 'Breeding with him was unforgivable.'

'Your wife, Rathmandria, did the right thing.' Ravaque said to comfort him. 'Killing them was the only way to cleanse your line of such filth.'

'Order will be restored to our household,' Belenus agreed firmly.

The red-and-gold-clad god kicked in the door. 'It will be, once we re-educate these ungrateful hordes as to their true place in the world—under our boot heels.' He strode inside.

Screams of agony erupted from within, mixed with Ravaque's laughter. Belenus ignored the weakness of blood loss and followed, and with a quick gesture the screams ended.

Ravaque threw him wry smile. 'You always spoil my fun,' he teased.

Belenus gestured above, towards their destination. 'Time presses,' he explained.

Ravaque distastefully kicked the ash of his victims off his boots.

Belenus ascended the stairs from the foyer, trying not to count the drifts of ash, and ignored his blood trail.

The Vault was opulent, it had been carved from stone of various colours. Inlaid in the floor was the icon of the Host, the mimic octopus. The walls were covered with murals depicting the Host, the thousands-strong war band of the Havilah, on their prior returns.

Gargantuan beasts of legends and nightmares depicted violent correction of the status quo. Titans and dragons lay waste to armies and krakens tore ships asunder. Innocents died by the thousands. Every previous revolt by the lesser races had resulted in slaughter by the Host.

This was the price paid for a technologically superior race to maintain the upperhand.

Another explosion rattled the windows, and Belenus glanced out. The building was vibrating with the explosions, and the multi-coloured lightning was almost constant.

'Come, Belenus,' Ravaque called once more, 'stop fretting. The Host will end it. We can start over with fresh stock. It is not as though the fae are equal to a Havilah.' He chuckled at the absurdity as he unlocked and entered the topmost room of the tower. Belenus followed without comment.

Vertical, rectangular benches of stone lined the walls, and a pedestal stood in the centre, a child-sized bifurcated amethyst egg atop it.

'What is this room?' Belenus studied the murals. They were somehow even more ominous than those in the foyer, and he felt a tingle at his nape. This was the first time he had been permitted to enter this chamber, despite his rank.

'This is where I summon the Host,' Ravaque explained, producing his signet and setting it into a recess. Luminescent squares appeared in the stone surfaces, a modern interface for an ancient computer. He tapped a few of these, and Belenus felt a deep hum vibrate through the stone beneath his feet. 'They go out to conquer other worlds, but return to maintain order,' Ravaque explained happily.

The amethyst was illuminated, and Belenus felt a throbbing from below that made his armour tremble.

'Once the crystal halves meet, the broadcast goes out,' Ravaque continued proudly. 'Wherever they are in the cosmos, they will hear it.'

The charred form of a gryphon careened past the window, and Ravaque gave it a foul glare. 'We will put an end to this. Perhaps wipe them all out,' he mused.

Belenus drew Ashril. 'I cannot let you,' he said softly.

Ravaque was surprised for the first time in a very long time. He blinked at Belenus and then he barked a laugh. 'And why not?'

Ashril luminesced, illuminating Belenus' stern face. 'Because my grandson lives,' Belenus announced. 'Rathmandria saw sanity after she murdered our daughter, and has fled with the child, abandoning her false godhood.'

'Why?'

'Because my grandson is as human as you and me, they all are.'

Ravaque knew that Belenus meant all of the slave races. It was the most important secret on Tuen: the Havilah were merely human, and the fae, elves, dryads and other non-humans were Havilah descendants, bred into specialties for service.

Ashril's hilt creaked as Belenus tightened his grip.

Ravaque laughed softly as it all fell into place. 'That's why the soft-hearted quick-kills, and why you wished to accompany me. To get in here.' He gestured at the pedestal and the computer panels that lesser education rendered as magical.

'This is wrong,' Belenus said quietly.

Belenus caught the wicked glint in Ravaque's eye, just before reaching hands became talons, a snarling mouth stretched into the fanged maw of a dragon, and a jet of sparkling blue light spewed from the beast's mouth. Belenus parried the beam with Ashril, then caught the beast's teeth with his blade and threw the monster aside.

'We aren't gods,' he shouted at Ravaque, and only received a snarl in reply. Ashril throbbed with light, and the dragon roared in pain, pinned down by tendrils of fire that tore off chunks of Ravaque's mass into blue particles, reducing his overall size.

Ravaque's will was powerful. He pushed back against the net, forcing Belenus to focus on maintaining the entrapment. He writhed and roared, broke free, and went for Belenus' throat. The silver armour saved Belenus. The teeth and claws left sizzling scratches across its surface. Clearly, their very touch would be lethal.

Belenus summoned a circle of light about himself, which threw off the dragon and pinned him to the stones once more. Belenus' vision swam, and one foot skidded in his blood. He was focusing on tearing the form from Ravaque, reducing him to merely a man once more, but the god of war was having none of it.

A blast of energy shot from the dragon's mouth and tore off Belenus' helm, disintegrating it, and tearing off half of the roof. The coruscations of light overhead mixed with the intimate battle in the tower. The side of Belenus face and neck was bloodied from where the beam had clipped him. His black hair still smouldered, and the wound in his side now stained all of his left leg crimson. With a tremendous effort of will, he was keeping Ravaque pinned.

However, the two halves of the summon crystal were inching closer, and Belenus knew he had to stop the countdown, whatever the cost. Belenus' muscles trembled, and for a moment his will almost faltered.

A life as a god was a good life to live. He would live millennia, and because of the use of the Seat of Heaven he was far more powerful than he would have been otherwise. Could he truly give that up? Could he live as a mere man, digging in the mud for food?

A flash of bright blue eyes beneath a shock of soft black baby hair flitted across his vision, and he had his answer.

Belenus glanced at the crystal halves, his limbs trembling and his strength failing, and then back at the raging dragon. No, he could not live like that.

Belenus sent a command through his sword and saw the net change from blue to pink lightning. He disconnected from the magic net and ran for the pedestal.

The dragon triumphantly tore free of the pink net in a matter of seconds, and lunged across the room, talons gouging into the stone as he roared after the silver-clad man. A ball of rotating energy formed in his open maw, one that would obliterate Belenus and not his summon crystal.

And then it went out. Ravaque coughed, and looked down at his dragon talons in confusion. His lower body had become stiff, hard to control, and as he looked he realised what Belenus had done to him. He could not comprehend that one he had trusted would do this to him.

Stone. Belenus was turning him to stone. It took longer on a Havilah, but it worked nonetheless.

Belenus was frantically pawing at the pedestal for some mechanism he could use to stop the contact of the two summoned crystals, a failsafe, or fuse to pull. He could find nothing.

Ravaque dragged his fossilising body towards his foe, snarling his hatred for this traitor.

Belenus was so intent upon preventing the summon mechanism that he did not realise he was in jeopardy until he was snatched up in the fanged dragon's maw. He screamed as Ravaque bit down on him, once, twice, denting and puncturing his armour. He could not free himself. He did not try.

The amethyst halves were almost joined, and in that split second the unbreakable diamond blade of Ashril slammed down between them. The summon mechanism ground itself to a silent halt, and as Ravaque stretched his mouth to scream his defeated rage, the last of the stone overtook him, forever frozen in impotent fury.

Belenus gingerly extricated himself from the mouth of the stone dragon and collapsed in a clash of metal at the base of the pedestal, his blood pooling on the cold stone. He would not leave this building, he knew, but he was content.

Belenus felt a heavy crump shake the foundations of the mountain. Every remaining window shattered, and he felt the blast wave of power tearing down the mountain and ever outwards. He realised the Seat of Heaven, the main technological source of the false gods' powers, had been detonated by the Free Races, and he smiled.

It would cost the fae dearly to contain the blast, but his grandson now had a future. The Havilah, who had shed their false godhood, planned to share their technology, and would nurture the remains of the fledgling free nations.

And the Host would never be called to return.

Boulders rained down upon the city. The mountain had disappeared into a mushroom cloud, darkening the skies, and the pyroclastic cloud from its annihilation buried the city of Isiridil, and Belenus.

A MORNING OF MANY

Maria Parenti-Baldey

Do you sometimes wish journeys were a tinsy bit more interesting?
Not just in life, maybe somewhere like on a train or a plane, or in this instance a bus.
Do you yearn for a morning with some five spice and a dash of chilli?
The front row seat of a bus is one such place.
Actually, it's one my favourites.
It has the best view, the vantage point.
It's the hottest seat on wheels.

'Fasten your seatbelts!' old Ted yells, with a wink and a nod.
As he steers, I peer round and round the roundabout, and into the third exit.

A steeple of trees stretches high, high above dipping their
heads in the clouds.
Aah, if only I had a portable transporter,
to jettison up, up and up away from this chaos of cars.
'Whoa! Why suddenly so chilly?
And why am I straddling a branch?
And why so many faces upturned, necks craned waving
from the bus below?
Cars, buses and trains jammed – eyes upwards.
And here I am perched with my frilliest knickers on show.

Thump! Bump.
Back into my front row seat I land.
The aisle passengers take a giant leap frog back.
'Witch,' some whisper. 'Sorceress.'
The row behind has emptied.
Old Ted throws me a grin.

Up ahead, I see passengers lining the usual footpath,
    watching, waiting.
    Up flies their hands to signal 'hail'.
    I just wish we could fly straight past them,
    instead of stopping at every other block.
    'Hey! Wait! Stop! Wait for us Driver!!

The bus zoomsed straight past them.
It's heading towards that Highrise.
'Holy smoke-a-roly! Stop Ted! Stop!'

Old Ted's eyes are wild as he steers straight ahead.
'Turn Ted! Turn!'
The left side of my face is plastered flat against my seat
window,
My peripheral vision spies darkening cauliflower clouds.
The front window is splattered in feathers and crimson.
Lightning strikes the city below. Thunder grumbles like
a V8 engine.

'Take me back Ted! Take me back!
But this is outrageously your best bus ride ever.

I know what you're thinking. I'm not as young as I used
to be.'
He tips his hat and grins.
Ted maneuvers the bus, dropping back onto the busway,
as if we had never left.
The cumulonimbus cloud rains rain, washing away the red
smudges and feathers.

Next stop.
A family of southern cassowary await.
Up flies their triangular bill to signal the obligatory 'hail'.
Brake. Screech. Stop.
On they alight.
Stomp. March. Stomp.
The aisle passengers squash further to the back.

I'd get further back too if I could. Those big birds are fairly pongy.

Sprouting through the bus roof is the mushroom shaped crown of the emergent layer.

A layer of leaves and branches canopy across the roof ceiling.

Wonderous cool, crisp fresh mist swirls, chilling.

The aisle passengers are standing on seats.

The understory has little sunshine. Instead tree ferns, tree frogs, slithering snakes and insects dominate.

All passengers are far above the dark forest floor of decaying pungent leaves as the cassowaries nibble and forage.

'Ouch!'

A gray-brown helmet erect like a horn bobs up and down on my lap.

He has pecked bits of my mushy banana left from breakfast.

His two red waffles dangle from his neck like mistletoe at Christmas.

The horned cassowary bobs his head up and pecks at the red stop button.

Ding Ding

Off they trundle retreating, taking the rainforest with them.

Far, far away from the cueing cars and gagging grey smog.

Old Ted winks and nods.

I straighten my hat and inhale my sprig of lavender.

Brake. Jerk. Fling... Stop.
'Hey Ted, Take it easy!'
A car just cut us off.
My knee jams hard against the front board.
Not a word slips from ole Ted.
'Pull your head in donkey breath?' I yell.
'HeeAwh! HeeAwh!'
Clutching the lamp post is the car driver atop a donkey.
'HeeAwh! HeeAwh!'
'That's what you get for cutting the bus off you wank... .'
Oops! Best not say anymore.

Last Stop!
A young woman stands waiting.
Her small tee-shirt is far too small.
That used to be me, many, many moons ago.
Do you remember Ted?
Yes I was hot to trot, back in those days.
Old Ted arches his brow.
Maybe not that hot, but at least I could trot.
'A distraction some Mother's did say.'
Oh dear, that old bloke donged his head on the mailbox.
Ouch that lady in stilettos stubbed her toe.
'Ah yes, I was a beauty once.'

Cough
Her white linen hanky stains - a slight red.
Cough Cough

'Best get me back Ted.'
Ow! Me back. Damn me gammy knee.

'You've outdone yourself today Ted Dearest.
Never a boring ride when with you.'
'Far more five spice than chilli this time, Ay Ted.
Save the front seat for me again tomorrow.'

'How will you get out this time Mabel?'
'Don't you worry about that Ted. You leave that part to
me.'

THE CLOUDBURST

Robert Walmsley-Evans

Aberforth slid the neatly cut animal skin onto the small writing desk. A thin bone stylus lay between his fingers. He tapped the stylus against his chin and gazed out the window over the ocean. Heavy black clouds rolled in, and the surf became more violent. Out of the corner of his eye, he watched the people of the beachside village scramble to get in from the encroaching storm. Their panicked screams and shouts echoed around the cove.

Aberforth placed the stylus on the skin. Once he had finished his writings and signed his name, he stretched and gazed at the celling. He stood rolling his shoulders as he stretched his legs around the dwelling, rummaging about his little house. He spied the air-pressure instrument he was looking for and examined it. He turned the handle with practiced precision.

Click. The cogs started to turn on their own, and he watched as the dial quivered. The device was connected to a synoptic sensor that slowly turned in the wind outside.

'Hmmm, it's going to be a serious storm.'

He clasped his calloused hands together before fingering his signet ring, lost in thought. *Why did the villagers run from the storm? It was simply power, nothing more, nothing less. If the storm wished, it could destroy the village. The houses up on the hill had no chance of withstanding anything.*

I don't wish to use my power, he thought. He was dangerous. He couldn't be trusted. The villagers knew this. At least the old ones did. Aberforth would be destroyed, and the villagers would be destroyed if he helped, or if he didn't.

He shook his head in disbelief and scratched at his overgrown beard. A knock at his front door pulled him from his thoughts and he opened the old, splintered door. *One day I must repair this, he thought.*

'Ouch!' He tried to pluck the splinter from his throbbing finger with his teeth. He glanced around quickly, seeing no one. Flustered now, Aberforth turned to go back inside.

Woof.

Was that a bark he heard? There was a tug on his trenchcoat.

'Hey, sir, down here.'

Aberforth looked down. There stood a young boy and a dog. 'You're brave to be out here, child. There's a big storm coming.'

'You are here alone?' the boy said, leaning in to observe the interior of Aberforth's home.

'Yes. Your point being?'

'Well, you shouldn't be up here alone.'

'Don't worry about me,' Aberforth said, 'I have weathered many storms. You should be with your parents.' It was better if the boy died with his parents than with him.

Thunder shook the air around them.

'All right, kid, come on inside before that rain drenches you to the bone.'

The boy stepped over the threshold, shivering from the cold. The dog shook the rain from its coat.

'I'll get us something warm to drink.'

'Thank you,' the boy said. 'What's this here?' The boy was pointing to the desk behind the old man.

'A letter to a friend of mine.'

'He must be an important person. It's good-quality hide.'

'You could say that,' Aberforth said. He filled a clay cup with a golden liquid before passing it to the child. The steam carried with it a strong herbal aroma. 'So, what's your name, young man?'

The child took a gulp of the warming liquid. 'My name is Mordecai, and may I ask yours?'

'Aberforth.'

'Well, Aberforth, what makes this house safe when the beachside houses would be rattling by now?'

'Me.'

'You? How could that be?'

Aberforth waved a hand at a teapot. It quivered, levitated and landed on the table beside him.

Mordecai clapped with excitement. 'How did you do that?'

'I've had power from when I was a child. I was only ten when I came across a goblet made of onyx upon a stone in the rainforest to the north. A man in a dark coat approached me, smiled and said, "It's all right, boy, don't be scared. I come from a society of people whose task it is to protect this goblet. Its ability is to choose a storm breaker, a protector, if you will, whose job it is to protect against the impending tempest. It was foretold in legend that a storm will devour a town in one great cloudburst."

'I was young, frightened and intrigued. I didn't know what I was doing. What could I do? I wanted to be someone important and I was cold. I drank the warm, dark green liquid from the goblet. Wherever I went from then on, I brought destruction. Buildings caught fire when I touched them. Streetlamps melted as I walked by, and people became ill when I was near.'

Mordecai placed his cup on the table and pulled up a chair. His dog settled down beside him.

'I came across the fabled old wizard that had lived in this house before the village was even founded. I couldn't believe his house wasn't affected by my nearness, and my story unfolded from my mouth. The old man's expression grew grave with the telling of my story. He eased this ring off his own finger and gave it to me.' He showed the ring to Mordecai. 'I never take it off. It allows me to control my powers.

'I stayed with him for many years, learning, and also earning my keep so I was able to purchase the house from the wizard when he decided to retire. He walked into the woods one day and didn't return. I haven't heard from him since. The villagers stay away from me because their memories are long and they still remember the old times vividly.'

'Aberforth, no.' The young boy felt sorry for the old man. 'I like you, and I'm sure the village would, too, if you just gave them a chance.'

The sound of the waves outside became more violent.

'I wrote to the wizard to come back,' Aberforth said. 'I know that he won't receive it, but I wrote that letter all the same.'

Mordecai's dog barked.

Aberforth grimaced. He walked to the window, watching as the old houses rattled in the wind. 'It won't matter either way, for tomorrow there will be little remaining of our village.'

'No, it can't be. You have to help my village.' Mordecai dashed over to Aberforth's side. 'Please look inside you; you have to help. You have all this power. Prove to the villagers that you're no threat.'

'Why should I help? What is this village to me?'

The boy did not give up. 'My father is the head of a group of fishermen. They call themselves the Fishy Men. It is a good life down in the village. Day to day, I help my mother prepare meals before going down to play with the other children of the village. I sometimes trek in the hills. I go as far as the forest. Do you know Brown Bark Rainforest to the north? It is a tradition in our parts for young people to venture along a specific path. There are variants of the journeys that are taken, but all paths lead to the rainforest. I share my adventure stories with one of the other children who is too young to go trekking. One time I went too far into the rainforest. I ran into a gang of tree folk, who stole all my money and smacked me around. That's when my father taught me to fight. I'm getting pretty good. We all need each other. You need the fish that my family brings in, and we need you. Even isolated people who live on cliffs need to see that there are people who can help them when they need it.'

Aberforth sighed 'You are right, of course,' he said reluctantly. 'All right, this storm is intensifying. All magic is limited by nature, but my magic has the strength to counteract a cloudburst. It looks like the storm is getting stronger and stronger. I should go. You stay here. You can check how everyone's going with that telescope.'

'What telescope?' the boy said, looking around but not seeing where a telescope could possibly fit.

'That one.'

A telescope on a tripod materialised in front of Mordecai, who smiled.

'Here, kid, hold my ring. I shan't need it.'

Mordecai put on the ring. He looked at the insignia etched upon it—a stylised dragon with the shape of a star around it.

As Aberforth walked down the cliff and onto the beach, his nerves grew. He sensed Mordecai's eyes following his gait. *Here it comes*, he mouthed, looking towards the sea.

The rain stopped, but the waves grew. It was the worst storm in the village's history. Aberforth stared back at his house—even it trembled, but Aberforth shone. Yellow and blue particles floated away from his body. He knelt. The process stung his entire body and he screamed out in pain. Flesh fell away and disintegrated. He couldn't control himself.

I look like an otherworldly creature, he thought. As he looked down at his body, it morphed into an intangible form. The waves receded and the sun broke through the clouds.

Aberforth opened his eyes to see that his surrounds had changed. 'Where am I?' he said.

A voice echoed around him. 'You are in a place between worlds.'

'Which worlds am I between?'

'The physical world and the world we cannot see, the one of mystics, of magic. Pure magic. The world of me.'

An eagle swooped from above, landed and stood in front of Aberforth. The eagle grew and changed.

Aberforth grinned. 'It's *you*. The wizard. The one who helped me.'

'Yes, it is I.'

'Why am I here? Haven't I destroyed myself to save the village?'

'You are here because you need to be; besides, you are not quite human. You are more resilient than a simple human. You do realise that you don't look like other earthly beings. Your father may have been human, but your mother was a spirit of the forest.'

Aberforth stepped forward. He'd just about had enough.

The wizard raised a hand and said, 'Why are you so angry? I am merely spelling out the facts of the matter. There is no time for polite chat. The people representing me on Earth have become too powerful. They realise their strength. They are greedy, they want all power for themselves. I realise now that this is my fault. I introduced magic to the physical realm well before anyone was ready for it and my followers were overwhelmed, it appears.'

'You're a wizard. Can't you just click your fingers?'

'I retired to the rainforest, remember? When you retire you give up certain things as a wizard. Enough about me, though. A lot has changed since you went from Earth. Time changes quicker for them than for us. That boy that you gave my ring to is now a man.'

'I thought I had completed my purpose, which was to stop the great storm.'

'There is more to the storm than rain and waves,' said the wizard with a wave of his hand.

Aberforth's brows netted, his mouth contorted. 'What do you mean?'

'Just watch, wait and act when you need to. But also remember to act when you think you don't need to. By the way, I saw your letter, thank you.'

The wizard turned. Aberforth followed his gaze. The wizard waved a hand in front of them both.

A circular window of space appeared. It focused on an image of Mordecai lying on a wooden, splintered rickety bed. He was not a small boy anymore.

Mordecai opened his eyes when a knock at the door roused him. He rose to open it and smiled.

'Hello, Claire.'

'I see you've got your bags, but you're not even dressed.' She raised a brow.

Mordecai rubbed his eyes. 'Of course I am. All I need is a shirt and jacket, just wait a moment.' He was back within a minute.

Mordecai and Claire walked through the streets of the town, waving to the townsfolk as they passed.

'Are you looking forward to your first journey over the hills and into the rainforest?' Mordecai asked the pretty girl.

'Very much,' Claire replied. 'I have always wanted to go, and my first time will be with you, an added bonus.'

Mordecai smiled. 'It was terrible that you were sick for so many years. But now I can show you places that I have so far only told you about.'

They walked in silence to the first of the hills. Claire and Mordecai stumbled over rocky out crops and twigs that seemed to appear out of nowhere. They came to an aged wooden structure that looked like it should have been higher in the mountains, nestled in the snow. A wooden plank hung above the entrance. The writing scrawled across it read, *The Travellers Inn.*

Mordecai turned to Claire. 'Shall we stop for some lunch?'

'Yes, please. That was a longer walk than I'm used to.'

An old, grey-haired woman served them. Her clothes were torn and she walked with a limp, but there was wisdom in her eyes.

'Where are you two young people off to?'

'We're going into the Brown Bark Rainforest,' Claire said.

'Be careful. There's strange happenings in that forest you be going to. People have been known to change there and bad things live there.' The old woman turned and walked away.

'That was peculiar,' Mordecai said.

Claire kissed his hand. 'Oh well, we will be in the rainforest soon.'

Finishing their lunch, they paid the old woman and walked hand in hand into a nearby field.

'This is out of our way,' Claire said.

'Yes, I agree. However, it is about the journey and not the destination. Every trek is different because of this. It is still on the path, however, simply a longer route.'

Claire flashed a cheeky smile at Mordecai and they ran for a time across the field.

Aberforth flicked a finger, and a small rock bounced from his otherworldly place to land in front of the young couple.

Claire and Mordecai tripped and fell upon their backs, laughing.

Mordecai pulled the ring off his finger, and turned it over in his hands. 'Do you remember the story I told you about the man I met, the one who I said saved our town?'

Claire nodded, her eyes squinting in the midday sun.

'This is his ring. I miss him.'

'You know we never believed you.'

'I know, but if I remember it, surely it happened in some reality.' Mordecai replaced the ring. His love for

Claire raced through his blood, and he took her face between his hands and kissed her deeply.

'Oh, Mordecai, I do love you so.'

Mordecai stood, offering his hand. 'I, too, my love, shall we move on?

'Let's.' Claire stood.

They were at the entrance of the rainforest within the hour. The thick trees enveloped them as they stepped upon the lush grass. Dappled sun came through the canopy.

Claire looked around. 'It's beautiful. That woman didn't know what she was talking about.'

'It's true that it looks harmless, but that woman appeared to have a deeper understanding, a knowledge that we don't have.'

'Oh, you're so serious sometimes.'

The rainforest was dark, though serene. They entered. They walked past shrubberies and ferns. Birds chirped in tall trees, the vast canopy surrounding them.

Mordecai scratched his ring. It felt tighter on his finger.

'There is more to that ring than meets the eye,' Aberforth said, still watching intently.

'Did you say something?' Mordecai asked Claire.

'Me? No, nothing. Should we stop here a while?'

Mordecai nodded. They sat on a couple of logs.

'Here,' Claire said, 'I brought sandwiches.'

Mordecai took one. As he chewed, he saw two goblets materialise in front of them.

Claire's eyes widened. She gawked at the goblets. 'Such well-crafted goblets, and all the way out here. What's going on, Mordecai?'

He stared at the onyx goblets. 'I ... don't know,' he stammered. Could history be repeating itself, he thought.

Aberforth nodded with the knowledge that this was indeed true, but it wasn't the same, it was different.

A man in a black jacket came out from behind the tree, followed by a group of ten. Claire screamed as one of the people in the group grabbed her arm and pulled her into the forest.

'Claire! No! Leave her alone.' Mordecai struggled to get to her. 'What do you want with her?' he yelled.

'Oh, nothing, not yet anyway,' one of the men replied. 'You were friends with someone so powerful that they could stop the worst storm that had ever existed. We wish to have that power returned.'

'How can I give back what I don't have? Aberforth vanished and I don't know where he is.'

'There is another option. Drink from one of these goblets and you will receive the same powers, and then we will siphon them from you.'

'Why can't *you* drink from the cup?'

'We are not worthy.'

'Why are there two cups?'

'We like games. Drink from one, and you won't have to deal with the power or its consequences. Drink from the other and you will receive the power.'

'And what of Claire?'

'She's just insurance to make sure you go through with it.'

'Fine. I choose the third option.'

Mordecai's training ran through his mind. He jabbed one of the men in the sternum. Roundhouse kicked another. He felt one grab the back of his shirt. Mordecai turned and gave him a decent uppercut to the jaw. The other one struck him hard on the temple, making his head spin, and he fell to the ground. His vision blurred. He could taste the metallic taste of blood, but he clambered to his feet to block another strike. He threw a right hook. It landed on the mystic's cheek. Huh, my father taught me well, he thought.

He saw a twig grow out of the earth, grab one of the mystics and drag them away. There was only a handful left. He outstretched one hand, closed his eyes and thought about Aberforth and Claire. His ring shone brightly. The other mystics froze and fell to the ground.

Mordecai sprinted. He didn't know where he was going. A small, injured voice echoed behind him, 'You will not prevail.'

Claire was sitting on the ground with one of the mystics pacing in front of her. The young couple stared at each other.

The mystic made a noise in the back of his throat that slowly increased in volume. He grew into a beast on two legs, with razor-sharp claws and teeth. Eyes blood red. Shaggy fur grew thick around its brow and covered its body. It let out a deafening roar. It threw Mordecai to the ground like a ragdoll. The beast struck him with frenzied blows. Mordecai struggled. Scrambling free, he swayed, feeling dizzy. He stumbled forward, kicking the beast in the thigh. He drew the mystic into an arm bar and grappled it to the ground. He struck the beast. The impact made the mystic shrink back to its human form and it vanished.

Claire stood and ran to Mordecai.

They asked each other if they were okay and kissed.

'This ring is too powerful for this world.' Mordecai placed the ring onto a bolder and raised a nearby rock.

'Are you sure?'

He nodded, driving the rock onto the ring. He felt a shift in the air pressure.

Mordecai and Claire covered their ears as successive screams resonated from the mystics. The forest eventually fell silent, and they fell into each other's arms.

Mordecai exclaimed, 'Everything is back where it should be, in balance.'

JOSHUA'S END

Pamela Jeffs

My leg is throbbing with a searing, burning pain. I grit my teeth and dare to look down at the precipice that falls away from my uneven shelf of rock. How stupid of me to wander so close to the edge, so stupid. And no one even knows I am here.

I have fallen several metres and the dust carried with me still hangs in the air. I try to shift myself into a more comfortable position, but my leg is having none of it. I almost faint as another bright gush of blood floods down my calf and across my shoe.

I suck in a panicked breath, the sob leaches out into the dusk. I tighten my hands just above the wound and lean back against the cliff face. I try to focus my attention away from my pain, away from my fear of dying alone. I let my gaze travel out across the valley below. The fading light has painted the rainforest into a wrinkled blanket of dark greenery and shadow. I close my eyes, and feel the currents of cool air rush up the cliffs and brush past me. They carry with them the heady scent of damp vegetation.

A sound. I open my eyes and am met with a wash of starlit darkness. Where am I? How odd that I had fallen asleep without making a fire. Then I remember. Horror constricts my heart. My head swims. That's right. I am clinging to the side of a cliff.

Alone.

The sound visits again, the grinding of stone over stone. I turn to my left and see a glimmer of light outlining a dark rectangle of rock. A doorway?

The grinding continues. The light shifts. Yes, it is a doorway. It opens into the cliff. A shadow fills it, its darkness surrounded by a burning yellow-white light.

I know I have lost too much blood. My head is light and my hands are trembling. The shape moves toward me. I am afraid of it. Am I dead and this is the devil coming for me?

God knows I deserve it—to go to hell, I mean.

The body of the man I murdered, freshly buried in soil above, is enough confirmation.

I think.

I remember the shovel, the smell of clean fresh earth, and the metallic scent of blood tainting it. I can't remember exactly how I killed him, yet I know I did.

I am so dizzy, and it's so hard to remember the exact details.

The light from the doorway is hurting my eyes. Too bright. When I try to shuffle away from the light, the clotted blood covering my wound cracks. Another flood of warmth sheets down my leg and my stomach lurches sideways.

The shadow man pauses. I see his hand is on the door. The light reveals the nature of it, the colour of his skin. It's pale blue.

But isn't the devil red?

Then his cool hands are lifting me away from the rocks. I am aware, but only barely, of being carried through impossibly bright hallways. Strange music echoes in my ears. Soft. Lilting.

There is no breeze in this place and so I feel warm. The smell of the rainforest has changed, has become that of flowers and the wet scent of mossy places.

I hear voices. They are too high, too lyrical to be human. *'Poor man.'*

'It is he, is it not? The human who sits on the cliffs?'

Then a heavier voice, no less lyrical for its weight, rumbles over me. *'Yes. It is he. Let me pass.'*

I can smell dogwood, and I feel the sunlight's warmth playing across my skin. I open my eyes and stretch. For a moment I revel in the sweetness of a bright morning, then realise how close I am to the precipice. Memories come flooding back.

How the hell did I get here?

I was not at the top of the cliff.

I was below it, facing the prospect of a lonely death.

Yet somehow, impossibly, I am back where I started, back at the top. I sit up and scrabble to feel my leg. There is dried blood on my skin and a knotted cord of scarred flesh. But otherwise I am whole and healed. I glance about. I can see the torn edge of the cliff where I fell the evening before. Dark earth is exposed and there is a patch of grass missing. My satchel lies a few feet away from the wound in the stone and the earth. Next to it is a journal, pages fluttering in the wind. I crawl over to it.

And I see my words creeping across the pages, handwritten in black ink.

And Joshua lifted the shovel, pressing its dented edge into the fragrant ground. But even that good, clean smell could not absolve him of what he had done. He had murdered the man, and now the scent of the blood nearby ruined any beauty this lonely place could offer ...

I feel a rush of relief. It wasn't me. I hadn't hurt anyone. My protagonist was the murderer. Joshua. And I was in this remote place, alone, to write his story, to write my novel. I'd been taking a break when I had wandered too close to the cliff edge and fallen.

Then I remember something else.

The pale blue man.

The voices, the light and the music.

I drop the journal and am suddenly searching for the one who saved me. I look through the twisted tangle of rainforest behind me, past the lush grass and tumbled granite boulders. But there is nothing, nothing but my journal.

I turn back to look at it. As I do, the wind catches the pages and flips them to the last. There I see words scrawled across the paper in pale blue ink. I lean in to read them.

Your life was saved for the gift of your words. Finish the story, human. We of the mountains have been listening—we wish to hear how Joshua ends.

A TALE OF THE MOUNTAINS

Rachel Nightingale

When I think of forever, I think of the mountains, their blue eternity stretching away, unperturbed by the mist that whispers over them. In their silent slumber, the mountains know the mist is only the briefest of daydreams and is unable to conceal them for long beneath its shadowy veil. I see the trees of the rainforest stretching in a wave below me, the green melding and shifting in an endless whisper. I remember the mellow blue silence of the air. My memories colour the majesty of the landscape, painting it with my Welsh grandmam's lilting tones, rusty with age. She was forever, too. To my young eyes, and those of my sister, she was surely as old as the mountains we gazed at, wide-eyed as baby possums.

Our first trip to the mountains was on Grandmam's birthday. Her final one, we were to know later. Born and raised in Wales, she and Granda emigrated to Australia to make their fortunes in a young land, a land glowing with hope and prosperity. The unique beauty of the Australian rainforest tugged at their misty-dales blood, so much so that they moved to a tiny country town in the mountains, away from the heat and hurt of the uncontrollable, ugly city.

Our mam and our uncle Gwyn were raised in the peace of the mountains, but both chose a career in the city. The city—glittering and bold, noisy, and filled with its own neon wonder. I think it broke Granda's heart to lose both children to Sydney's flirtatious glitz. Even his gentle mountains could not console him over this betrayal. He died while I was still a baby.

Afterwards, Grandmam wanted to stay in her home, but Mam wouldn't have it. Live in the mountains on her own, with the icy winters tearing apart her final shreds of youth and strength?

So Grandmam moved in with us. We used to love sitting with her and listening to her stories. Such wonderful stories. I can understand now that she was pining for her mountains, and the shadows of her Welsh homeland, fading in her memory.

Grandmam's stories cast their spell on us. We loved the mountains and sensed their magic before we ever saw them. We could picture the dark little faerie folk of the Welsh foothills, and their Australian cousins, who tended the mist-laden trees and sprightly wildflowers of Grandmam's lost garden. I came to feel awe for the people who dared to live in such a wild, eternal country, and for Granda, too, though I never knew him. I came to believe that he and Grandmam had captured the magic of the mountains, drawing it into their hearts and lives as easily as they had in their beloved Welsh hills.

Grandmam told us how they had let the wildflowers and determined rainforest take over their garden instead of trying to impose their own ideas of cultivation. I learned to respect the Granda I had never known, and through him, a country I had never seen.

Where other children were raised on homemade cakes and biscuits, or coins and sweets, our treats were the stories Grandmam wove for us. Even when we were young she was very old, held together by her tales, her determination, and the eternal strength of the mountain that ran through her blood. We never saw her bustling around, baking or cleaning or buzzing with energy. She was frail and tired, but there was tranquillity within her. We were lucky to have the time with her that we did. It was long enough for her to instil in our receptive hearts the peace of her mystical mountains. She conjured dreams for us that remained with us long after her passing, imaginings that somehow became real.

As I grow older, I become sure that she knew how little time she had left. The relentless clock of mortality ticks within all our hearts, if we will only listen. It was for our sake as much as her own that she asked that we all go back to the mountains on her final birthday. Mam didn't want to go. She had always seen something frightening in their dark, misted grandeur. They were too big for her. She had lit her world with neon and shaken it up with noise to keep out the hints of forever. But my sister and I were so young. We could drink in forever with gasps of wonder, and still have room left over. We were prepared to see worlds beyond yesterday and tomorrow, beyond the ever-present unreality of real city life.

It was a long drive, longer than we had ever known at that stage of our lives. But we knew from Grandmam's stories that we were going to see pure magic, undiluted by trains and bricks and pollution-drenched broken hopes. To Mam it must have been a terrible chore, driving us back to her childhood, with its restrictions and powerlessness, and listening to Grandmam restoring to life a past Mam would rather forget.

We had lunch in a tiny restaurant that epitomised 'olde worlde' charm. It seemed, then, the height of grandeur. Now when I stop there for a coffee, forty years later, I can't help seeing the tacky souvenirs behind the counter, the chipped paint and the imitation bone-china plates. But somehow I also still see a lingering glow of magic dust. I don't come back often. Perhaps I'm afraid something will be lost if it becomes too familiar. But when I do, when I reach the mountain itself, it is as though I can still see the track of Grandmam's wheelchair blending with the ridges and furrows of the ancient rocks, dry now, but filled with rainwater that first time.

The mountains do not seem as dangerous now, either. When gusts of wind push at me, they don't feel menacing, but comforting. Even when I visit during a storm, when lightning tears across the rocks and shreds the mist, revealing what has been thinly veiled, I feel a strange comfort. Even in the brooding, shifting clouds—layer upon layer of them—I see eternity. When I was a child, the clouds never moved. They seemed steadfast and strong, always in one place. Only the mists moved, dancing with capricious zephyrs. Now the clouds seem ephemeral as thought. Even the storm will end. I see fragility in everything but the mountains themselves.

That first trip, though, that was the first time I noticed how tiny and fragile Grandmam was, like one of Mam's fine porcelain plates. But I hadn't known death yet, that I could remember. I thought Grandmam would endure. Even as her hands shook, she seemed part of this solid, forever world. I see now that she was the mist, drifting away from us in the same way her voice was snatched by the wind.

She told us her best story then, the one to haunt me in my romantic years, a story with a sad truth behind it; her personal tragedy, and Mam's, too. But she told it just as she had any other, her voice wafting in and out of the nearby clouds. I never noticed the tears in Mam's eyes throughout the telling, or her quiet, persistent 'That's enough, Mam' breaking in every so often. Yet I hear it now, so clearly, a well of grief unnoticed at the time.

I never thought there could be any truth to this tale, with its capricious magic that tossed our braids and shook our dresses. But Grandmam's broken voice told true.

'Aye, she was a beautiful girl, was Linnet. Such long, rich chocolate hair and jewels like the sea for eyes. And such golden skin. She was like a faerie changeling. It was no wonder Dale loved her so. Ah, he was a brave lad, noble and proud' — and here Mam gasped and said, 'No, Mam, not this story' — 'and such a great heart it would seem all creation was there for him to cherish. He had a family who loved him dearly, and a brother and sister he would play with patiently, though they were much younger and right nuisances to a boy of that age. And Linnet, why she was almost part of the family, too, for she had only an old da, and he cared little what she did.

'Together they roamed this forest often, taking long walks among the trees, finding little treasures to bring home to Dale's mam, flowers and pretty stones and the like. And since she had Dale's heart, Linnet had to give him something in return, so she gave him a gold chain, very old and valuable, with an even older key on it. Linnet didn't know what the key was for, and nor did her da, for it was older than he could remember. But she said it were the key to her heart, and that were enough.

'They were to be married. Dale's mam made Linnet a beautiful dress, and the preparations were all done. Then, a few short days before, they went walking together, to talk about their future. It were a lovely day, the clouds tumbling about like rollicking puppies, the mountains seeming close enough to whisper their secrets. There were a light rain, which made the colours melt over the scene like someone were mixing all the blue and green paint in the world over the crags.

'Linnet and Dale were walking along a shady path in the valley at the foot of the cliffs when a rumbling like thunder filled their ears. They thought the rain was threatening, though the clouds were not dark and frowning but dancing white. They began to look for shelter. Then rocks began to fall around them. The cliff face was collapsing, and they were caught underneath. They ran, hand in hand, but they were too slow for the crashing rocks. Then a wondrous thing happened. The magic of the mountain surrounded them, singing in their ears. A blue mist enfolded them, lifting them into the air and changing them. Each felt their body melting into a new shape, a shape that meant freedom.

'Linnet gave a joyous cry, and her voice rang out through the valley. Their hands, touching, became feathers on long, arching wings. The mist no longer needed to hold them, for they were airborne, gliding above the avalanche and reeling through shafts of golden sun, their cries echoing and ringing. Linnet was grey and sleek, but still with her beautiful sea-eyes watching the world pass beneath her. And Dale was the same grey underneath, but his wings were of the purest gold, from Linnet's chain and key. They flew with the freedom of birds above the rocks that trapped secrets beneath their terrible weight.'

Mam broke in then. 'You know that's not what happened. Dale and Lin were killed in the rockfall. There was no magic. I hate these mountains for taking my brother. Making up stories doesn't take away the pain. I won't let you fill my children's ears with such rubbish.'

Grandmam shut her eyes, rocking back and forth just a little. 'I know what I know. And I feel no pain.'

At that moment a sunbeam washed across Grandmam's face, like the gentle tranquillity after a storm. I believe she really felt no pain at that moment. She opened her eyes to the gentle light and I could see the magic of the mountains shining out of them. Before Mam could say anything else, we saw, flying towards us on a golden beam of sunlight, two birds of a gentle grey. They drifted up from the valley and flew so close we could see every feather. At the last moment they wheeled gracefully off to the right. The sun shone off the beaten gold wings of one bird. And in that moment of nature's grace, I believed in eternity.

THE LOST

Christine Kelly

The football soared between the two tents, the designated makeshift goal posts for the impromptu game of Aussie rules. It thumped into a mountain-ash tree before rolling further into the surrounding rainforest.

'Goal!' The roar echoed in triumph through the campground at Aire Crossing in the southeast of Victoria.

'Oi, dinner's nearly ready,' a short woman with dark hair and doe-like eyes shouted from one of the camper vans parked nearby, a small child of about five clinging to her leg like her life depended on it.

'Dee, Helen, bring the kids, we'll start setting up,' the woman called.

They packed up their camping chairs and herded the children who could toddle about on their own toward the camper.

'Someone go find the others. They've gone down thataway.' She indicated a park sign that pointed down a path. The sign had an arrow and the words *Cora Lynn Cascades* engraved into the wood. 'Hurry them up, will ya?' she said. 'The food will go cold.'

The men groaned — all but one. A tall man with eyes of eerie grey nodded to the tiny woman and set off in the direction she indicated.

'Thanks, Dean,' she called after him.

'Roped you in, did she?' A stout man with thinning hair swaggered up to Dean, pulling on a T-shirt. 'She's good at that, reminds me of ...' He trailed off with a wince, observing his friend's downcast expression and tense shoulders. 'Sorry, Dean,' he murmured, resting a hand on his mate's shoulder.

'It's okay, Ian, it's been five years, I just ... around famil ... I just miss Em.' The last was whispered. 'She loved coming here. It just brings back the good old days, ya know.' He straightened. 'Now I better go find this lot.' He smiled before heading down the path to the Cascades.

'Hey, look for a footy down there, one of the kids dropped it,' Ian called, as he watched his best friend disappear past a sign warning walkers to stay on the trail at all times.

'Will do,' came the reply.

Dean made his way down the densely shaded path and into the wet greenness that was the Great Otway National Park. The trail was enclosed by ferns and trees that seemed to touch the sky. The crunch of gravel beneath his feet seemed loud in the silence, broken only by the hum of insects, and the twitter and flutter of birds in the trees. It filled Dean with a sense of peace he hadn't been able to achieve in a long time.

Five years, to be exact.

Not since his wife's death had he been able to come to this magical place, which had featured in so many of their happiest memories. It was still the same, as though time had stood still here, and if he listened hard enough he could swear he heard her voice, her laughter, echoing through the trees.

The grief still burned in him like a hot iron to his chest, and he ached constantly from holding in his screams of loss ... and guilt. But now, in this forest, where so many memories existed of the woman he loved, he could breathe again.

A low murmur pulled him from his thoughts, and he glanced around, searching for the source, realising it must have come from the group he was looking for.

'Alex,' he called, testing to see if there was anyone nearby, or if he had been so lost in his memories that the sound of voices had only been a figment of his imagination.

Silence.

Thick and heavy, with the density of the forest.

Dean breathed in deeply, allowing his eyes to slip closed as he stopped walking and simply stood in the soft embrace of the forest, losing himself to the magic, even if only for a moment. He let the day fade away, and the cool of the forest wrapped around him on every side.

'Help!' The cry was so faint he almost didn't hear it. He blinked his eyes open, turning on the spot, confused.

'Help!'

This time the call was louder, although still faint. It was definitely real, and the caller sounded very young.

He stilled, surveying the area, the path, the trees, attempting to gauge the direction the call had come from.

'Help me!' The call came from his left, beyond the trees, and without a thought or care for safety, *he stepped off the path*.

It felt like he had been walking for hours, but when he glanced at his phone, he realised it had only been twenty minutes.

He called out to the voice, attempting to pinpoint the location. He didn't seem to be getting any closer, and always, just as he was about to give up and turn around, he would hear the child again, begging for help.

'Hello,' Dean called again, pausing to glance around, worry beginning to nag at him.

He knew he shouldn't have left the path—there were warning signs everywhere—and now he wasn't sure he knew exactly where the path was.

He stood to his full height and called out again. 'Is anybody there?'

Silence.

With a shake of his head, he turned around to attempt to make his way back to the path when he heard the voice again, only this time it was much closer.

Almost beside him.

He spun, expecting to see a child standing behind him, but found no one.

'I'm over here. Help me, please.' The voice held a sob.

He spun in the voice's direction and sprinted, knowing that this child was in desperate need of help and comfort, and he was *this* close to finding them.

He was running and fighting his way through ferns when the first inkling hit him that all was not right.

It may have been the sensation of falling that tipped him off.

Or the darkness that suddenly eclipsed his world.

The last thing he thought was that he should not have left the damned path.

When Dean regained his senses, the first thing he noticed was that he was wet and cold, mind-numbingly cold.

The second was that someone was sniffling close by, as though trying to control the urge to cry, but couldn't quite manage to stop it completely.

With a pained groan, he sat up, noticing he was on a bed of hard, water-smoothed rocks in a rainbow of colours. The rocks were strewn in a crescent shape, in what appeared to be a sinkhole.

He grumbled and cursed to himself as he checked for injuries, finding a rather large egg on the back of his head that ached with a pounding intensity that would put a hangover to shame.

Naturally rounded, the sinkhole resembled a large bowl, ferns and trees clung to the sides with stubborn dexterity. Old fallen trees rested against the walls in a parody of an upside-down forest, partially submerged in their plunge into the cool depths of the sinkhole.

What little sunlight there was hit the far wall in a burning orange glow, while casting the rest of the sinkhole, which Dean now realised was a cave, into shadow.

Only now, in the shade, he knew it would get real cold fast. He was already wet from his tumble into the sinkhole, night was falling and all he wore were jeans and a thin T-shirt. Hardly enough to keep him warm, especially in a cave, he thought. He waited for his eyes to adjust as he surveyed his home for the night in the quickly fading light of dusk.

His eyes finally adjusted properly to the darkness of the cave and widened at the size of it.

There'd been no signs of human interference in this area, no fencing around the edge of the sinkhole like there were with other fall risks in the forest. *Although if I'd stayed to the path I never would have needed a fence, he thought.*

Dean wondered if anyone had seen this cave. It was a treasure trove of plant and animal life, and he was pretty sure those were indigenous paintings on the walls.

A sniffle interrupted his thoughts, the same kind of sniffle he had heard upon wakening, before he had become entranced by his surroundings.

Narrowing his eyes, he studied the rapidly lengthening shadows, and the many nooks and crannies of the cave, before making his way further in, searching for the source of the sniffles.

He didn't have to go far. The tiny creature emitting the miserable sounds was hidden behind a large boulder not far from the entrance of the cave. Her pink T-shirt was damp and, while her little legs were covered by jeans, her feet were shoeless. A wild tumble of chestnut curls fell around her shoulders, and her cheeks were pale and looked cold.

'Hey, little one,' Dean cooed to the small child, *you couldn't be more than five if you were a day,* he thought. Her dove-grey eyes, which had previously been screwed tightly closed, flashed open.

Taken aback at the sight of eyes that almost mirrored his own, Dean took a deep steadying breath to control the emotions tumbling through him.

She shrank away from him for a moment as he settled down opposite her, not quite trusting him enough to let him nearer. At least she seemed to be in good shape and uninjured.

The wonder of the cave forgotten, he sat in silence for a few more moments before deciding he needed to do something to occupy himself, and try and keep them both warm, if not fed, for the night.

'I'm going to find some wood and attempt to start a fire, do you want to help me?' Dean gently asked the little girl, who still studied him warily.

After a long moment, finally she nodded.

She clambered to her feet before making her way to the edges of the cave to collect the smaller twigs that had fallen into the sinkhole. Dean collected bigger pieces of wood he could find that were mostly dry and dragged them back to a bowl in the rock floor of the cave, which would make a perfect fire pit.

He was not a smoker so he didn't carry a lighter. *Oh well,* he thought, *the old-fashioned way will have to do.*

As the cold encroached further into the cave, and the blanket of darkness descended, he set to rubbing sticks and wood together. He hoped those half-remembered video lessons years before on YouTube would suffice.

It took a while, but after a few splinters and the unexpected aid of his young companion, he was able to get first a spark and then a flame to catch in the kindling.

'Mummy will be looking for me.' The whisper took him by surprise as he reclined against one of the large boulders littering the cave. He was beside the little girl, who had seemingly decided he was trustworthy enough to speak to now.

He wondered which of the campsites she was from. The group he had arrived with had taken over half the campsites, and he knew she wasn't one of the many kids they had brought along.

'I will get you back to your mummy, little one,' he promised, putting his arm around the small child, who, shivering, willingly snuggled into his side as she tried to get warm, even though the fire roared away merrily in front of her.

'Alima.'

Dean glanced down at where the mumbled word had come from. Her small head was buried in his chest.

'Sorry?' he said.

The child lifted her head and met his gaze steadily. 'My name, Alima,' she said.

'Ahhh.' Dean nodded. 'Nice to meet you, Alima, and I promise to get you back to your mummy.' He smiled down at the child beside him, a pang tightening his chest.

'Now, did you know your name is Arabic? My wife was an Arab and she taught me a few words. "Alima" translates roughly to "skilled in music" or "sea-maiden",' he informed the child seriously. 'Are you either of those? I have my suspicions that you may be a sea-maiden.'

Alima giggled up at him. 'What's a sea-maidern?' she asked, pronouncing maiden with a hard 'r'.

Dean pretended to think for a moment. 'Well ... a sea-maiden is like a little mermaid, a little girl with a fish's tail, and she lives in the ocean,' he informed her before narrowing his eyes at her. 'I think you are a sea-maiden. Did you pull me out of the water, by any chance?' he asked, pretending to study the muscles of her little arms.

High-pitched giggling filled the cave. 'No. You are too big,' she said cheekily.

Dean pretended to be hurt. 'Are you calling me fat, Alima?'

She shook her head, a delightful smile spreading across her face when Dean raised a suspicious brow.

He cradled the little girl in his arms, his heart aching as he kept her warm. He would have loved to have a child of his own with Em. In fact, they had been trying for one, and had been in their second round of IVF when the car accident happened.

He closed his eyes as the crushing guilt consumed him, and his arms tightened around the precious child in his arms to the point where she whimpered in her sleep. Loosening his grip, he remembered the night his world had imploded. *It had been raining ...*

Dean drove carefully as they made their way to the appointment that would tell them if they were pregnant, the window wipers squeaking back and forth on the windscreen as the rain pounded heavily on the car roof.

'I hope this time it worked,' Em murmured, her hands resting on her flat belly, and her thick black hair hanging around her face as she studied the road ahead.

He reached a hand over and rested it on his wife's belly, taking his attention away from the road for a second. 'It will,' he whispered, putting every ounce of hope and faith into those two words as he comforted his wife, who desperately wanted a child to call her own.

He had looked away for only a split second, but the jolt of the car and scream of metal had his head snapping back in horror as he crossed the intersection and collided with the other car.

Em screamed.

Dean jolted awake, deep breaths sawing through his chest as he came back to the present.

It had been years since he'd had that dream. It must be this place, he mused, as he looked down for the little girl he'd been cradling, only to jump up when he found her absent.

'Alima!' he called. He scanned the rocks around him before his gaze made its way back to the water with wary apprehension. *'Alima!'* he roared, and began racing toward the water.

'I'm here.' The girl's voice called from behind him when he was almost at the water's edge.

'Alima!' Dean exclaimed as he fell to his knees in front of her and snatched her tiny body up in a tight hug. 'What were you doing? You almost gave me a heart attack. Don't you ever do that again, I mean it,' he warned her sternly before rising to his feet, still cuddling the little girl.

'I found Mummy,' she exclaimed excitedly.

Dean looked down at her warily. 'Where was Mummy, Alima?' he murmured tensely, and watched as she raised a little finger and pointed excitedly toward the darkness at the back of the cave.

Of course. 'You went into the dark on your own?' he said, glancing back at the brightly lit sinkhole entrance, and then at the almost pitch darkness beyond the circle of boulders surrounding the fire pit.

'Yep. I could hear mummy calling me.' She nodded excitedly, and began kicking her legs and wiggling her body to be released. 'Let me take you to Mummy. She wants to meet you.'

'Alima, your mother can't be in the back of that cave —' Dean began.

'Come on, Dean,' she called, suddenly sounding further away.

Dean bound to his feet as the little girl raced into the darkness at the back of the cave. 'Alima!' he roared, and took off toward the darkness, which was rapidly swallowing up her tiny form.

For a small child she ran fast, and he was puffing as he made his way into the shadows at the back of the cave. 'Alima,' he called, stopping to listen.

'Mummy,' the childlike voice sang, and he began moving toward it, only to stop in horror.

'Alima.'

A voice had responded to Alima's call.

'Alima, I need you to come back here, right *now*,' he roared, as he suddenly went cold.

'But Deaaaannn, Mummy is here. She really wants to meet you,' the call came back.

Dean's heart pounded in his chest. He was uncertain of what he would find in the darkness, his mind running through all the horror flicks he'd ever watched with his wife, who had for some reason *loved* the damned things.

He knew this was the part where the hero always made the stupid decision to go into the darkness. He knew this was where they always died.

But he went anyway, because a little girl was calling his name and she needed him.

And so he put one foot in front of the other and proceeded into the blackness.

'Come on, Dean, hurry.' Alima's voice echoed through the dark tunnel, which was pitch black.

'Alima, honey, keep talking so I can follow your voice. I can't see anything,' he called back.

'Dean ...' a new voice reached his ears now. It was faint, and blended with the little girl's. She continued to call and encourage him further into the darkness.

'Hello?' he called, arms outstretched as he shuffled forward. The darkness was thick and heavy and he began to worry when Alima didn't respond. 'Alima!' he snapped.

'I'm right here,' she said beside him, a pout in her tone.

He reached out a hand and felt around until he touched her soft hair. 'Okay, stay with me,' he commanded through gritted teeth, not liking being in the dark.

He froze, a faint lilting chuckle reaching his ears.

'Alima, who is here with us?' he asked, fear making his heart pound as he prepared to scoop up the little girl and sprint back the way they had come. He didn't care if he was cut and bruised when he got back to the light.

He would keep this little girl safe.

'Mummy is here,' she whispered, confused. 'Dean, why do you have your eyes closed?'

Dean tensed as he realised his eyes were indeed closed, though he had no memory of ever closing them, before slowly blinking them open.

Bright blinding sunlight greeted him, and he heard the chuckle of a nearby gurgling stream and the song of birds in the trees filling the air.

And a scent.

A scent that filled him with peace.

The scent that had died with his wife.

A small hand fitted into his and he glanced down to see a brightly beaming Alima by his side.

'Alima, what did I tell you about running away?' he muttered, before falling to his knees and crushing her in a hug.

Releasing her, he stood and glanced behind him at the dark entrance of the cave, which seemed to shimmer and waver in the clear air. 'Okay, we're outside, where is your mother?' he asked, turning back to the little girl, who watched him seriously.

She pointed to his left and he turned to meet the mother of his tiny friend.

'Hello, Dean.'

'Em?'

One week later ...

'There still has been no sighting of Melbourne man, Dean Adams, after he disappeared on a camping trip with friends in the Great Otway National Park at Aire Crossing, a popular campsite in Victoria.

Mr Adams was known to be grieving for his wife, Emuna Adams, who passed away five years earlier. The investigation is continuing, and police urge anyone with information to please come forward ...'

KEEPER OF THE FLAME

June Perkins

Breakaway connections
to ancestral glass.
Shake away attachment
all these things will pass.

Run away from secrets
In canopies be tearless.
Burn your spirit's wick
to the last be fearless.

Pace yourself to run
to forests bathed in light.
Steel yourself for sorrow
soften up its might.

Toss all your regrets
to the distant tundra.
Waltz your way to wisdom
Chase away the umbra.

Angels sowing splinters
make the heartless weep
but birth you into green
with mysteries they keep.

Hear ghosts of the forest
calling out your name.
willing you to friendship
You are the Keeper's flame.

RAINFOREST SPRITES

Katrina Rutgers

Modern Day Plague

Deforestation is clearing Earth's forests on a massive scale, often resulting in damage to the quality of the land. Forests still cover about 30 percent of the world's land area, but swaths half the size of England are lost each year.

The world's rainforests could completely vanish in a hundred years at the current rate of deforestation.

—The National Geographic Society, 1996–2015

'The warmer weather always tends to bring the humans out, and so many little ones with their precious toys.' Zanna smiles in grim satisfaction.

Foster agrees. 'This has been a most productive weekend, Zanna. The new recruits will please Avery.'

Gathered around the pair, deep within the mountaintop rainforest in Lamington National Park, are an assortment of grubby toys and torn little blankets. Previous weekends had been fraught with gale-force winds, pelting rain and one devastating hailstorm. Not conducive to tourists in the least.

'Sammie ... Sammmmie.' Plaintive sobbing ensues, echoing through the darkening rainforest high above the quaint, friendly town of Canungra and its surrounding farmlands.

A man is seen retracing his steps along the timber treetop walk. His eyes flicker rapidly from one spot to the next. He kicks at a cluster of leaves. Peers often over the side of the path into the lush foliage. Shines his phone torchlight into the deepening shadows. A grimly set mouth and a furrowed brow, along with his hasty movements, all indicate the importance of his mission.

By now the sobbing has faded into the distance.

With the daylight all but gone, the man reappears, plodding his way back while swearing under his breath and shaking his now dark mobile phone. 'Bloody useless thing.'

Momentarily it looks as if he will be tossing the 'bloody useless thing' into the shrubbery, but then he shoves it into his jacket instead. The man jumps and looks around with an alarmed expression. He hastens his step to depart in the same direction as the upset child and the female.

'I must remind you not to talk while the humans are so close, Zanna.' Foster's elfin look is serious, and his hands glow softly around a faded blue piece of cloth printed with a bear's head.

'Sorry, Foster, but could we not have managed to get these back to the human children tonight?' Zanna's look is more feminine. They are exquisite creatures. Petite, four foot high-ish, with a glowing tanned skin, long limbs, and the most delicate crystal-clear wings. They are typical of the ethereal rainforest sprites.

'No, we need to ensure the spell is woven in perfectly. We wouldn't want any problems.' Foster's hands are busy fluttering in a circular motion around the cloth. Sparks zing, lighting up the immediate area like miniature fireworks. 'It is imperative we get these children spellbound while they are unable to communicate effectively.'

'Of course, you are right. And your idea of casting a sleeping spell on the children will prevent their noisy emissions disturbing the locals.'

'Emissions? I think the humans say "crying".' Foster is staring intently at the iridescent bubble that has formed around the grubby cloth, glittering now with golden sparks. Abruptly the bubble dissolves, and with a few final flickers the cloth lands gently in his hands. 'It feels right now. We will check all the items in the morning before replacing them for the humans to find. We don't want any of those pesky possums running off with them. These enchanted items will remain with the humans to prevent them from becoming part of the human greed element destroying our ancient rainforests.'

On entering the motel room, the man is surprised at how silent it is. He had made one last-ditch effort to locate the missing Sammie by stopping by the resort's reception desk to inquire if someone had perhaps handed it in. The polite young receptionist had seemed most sympathetic, but had informed him that the only lost property was a pair of sunglasses.

Isabella is sitting at the tiny dining-room table, with their little boy, Zach, on her lap. The spoon she is holding has some sort of orange mash on it and she is trying in vain to shovel it into the boy's mouth. 'I don't understand what's wrong with him.' Her voice is higher than usual.

He shifts under her gaze and reaches up to rub the stubble on his chin. Adam never shaves on weekends.

'He won't touch his food, and he hasn't cried or spoken since we left the rainforest walk. Why isn't Zachie upset about losing Sammie? There's something very wrong. What should we do, Adam? He doesn't have a temperature.'

Statue like, Adam is staring at the unnaturally peaceful baby. Bizarre things are happening tonight. Missing Sammie, inhuman voices in the rainforest, and Zach asleep without his security teddy blankie. He shivers in recollection of the eeriness of the treetop walk as the light faded. Perhaps not sinister, but spooky nonetheless. A stark contrast to the fresh, peaceful feeling present during daylight hours, when the birds are warbling and scratching around in the deep foliage, and the sunlight shines thin rays through the dense canopy of trees.

'Are you listening, Adam? I'm worried.'

Adam snaps out of his trance. He moves swiftly to his Isabella. Crouching down, he reaches out to draw both his wife and child into his embrace. He feels Isabella relax into him, and Zach's warm baby softness under his chin fills him with love for their precious only child.

'Well, what should we do? Find a doctor?' Isabella's soft but worried voice finally urges Adam to answer.

'He seems to be fine. Look at his face—it's as though he's having a beautiful dream.' They both contemplate Zach's serene look, his even breathing, and his healthy baby colouring. 'I think we just tuck him into bed and let him sleep. It's a long and perilous drive down the mountain even in the daytime. I'd prefer not to drive it at night unless it's urgent.'

Placated, Isabella wipes Zach's mouth clean and lowers him into the portacot. She covers him warmly against the cold mountain air and kisses him goodnight. Adam, too, leans into the cot to lovingly stroke his son's wild red curls, which mirror his own, and plant a kiss on his chubby cheek.

'I'll call room service and order us some dinner and wine. We can have an early night and return to the walking path to find Sammie in the morning. How does that sound?'

Surprisingly, they all have a full night's sleep and wake at seven to a perfect autumn mountain day.

Zach is only slightly fretful. 'Find Sammie,' he repeats endlessly, like a broken record, as they all dress for the day.

Mums, dads and children are scattered on the forest walkway. A toddler by the name of Tom (according to his T-shirt) delightedly snatches up a threadbare teddy. A dark-skinned baby with a mop of kinky hair sucks her thumb contentedly while holding a faded pink piece of blanket to her chest. Adults are seen scratching their heads and looking decidedly puzzled.

Zach wrenches his hand free of Isabella's and makes his unsteady toddler way along the pathway, arms outstretched and babbling, 'Sammie, Sammie, Sammie.'

Adam and Isabella stare in disbelief as he triumphantly picks up Sammie, who has been resting against a moss-encrusted log no more than a few meters in.

'How did I miss that last night?' Adam wears an astonished look, and Isabella's expression mirrors his as they turn to each other.

'What's going on here?' someone says. 'Did your child lose their toy, too?'

Adults are questioning other adults. Mothers compare stories. Fathers relate their search efforts. They all have amazingly similar tales.

Deep within the rainforest, two sprites are congratulating themselves on a mission well accomplished.

Twenty-five years later

'Hey, Zach, is that a joey you have there? It sure was a helluva storm last night,' a male in his twenties says to the team leader, a ranger with an unruly mop of red hair.

'Hi, Tom, yes, unfortunately the mother was killed by a falling branch. Guess we'll have a full house at the hospital this week. I'm pleased we have so many volunteers coming up the mountain to help with the clean-up and play nanny to these little orphans.' Zach nestles the little bundle of fluff close to his chest. 'I'll take this one down to join the others and then meet you back here to organise the volunteers. The bus should be here very soon.'

'Righto, mate, I'll grab the vests for the volunteers.'

After an exhausting but productive day of clearing walking trails, and scouring the bush for any injured or orphaned wildlife and rehoming them at the animal hospital, Zach, Tom and an assorted mix of male and female volunteers are relaxing with beers or wine in hand. They have gathered on the porch of the hospital, all well rugged up with jackets, gloves and scarves. As usual, it is cold on this almost clear-sky autumn evening up on the mountain. The view is spectacular as the sun lowers itself behind the distant hills, with the sky morphing from aqua blue with soft grey clouds to golden orange, then a glorious lilac afterglow before full darkness descends.

A pretty African-Australian girl, Chloe, is relating a story that her parents had told her over the years about how they often used to come to the mountain for weekends of hiking and relaxing at this rainforest resort. How one time she lost her blankie along the walkway. She tells them she has always loved the lush forests, the birdlife and the occasional glimpses of forest creatures, such as tiny pademelons and bowerbirds, and once even a rare spotted quoll. Chloe relates how she moved to Canungra after finishing her veterinary nursing training in Brisbane, where she had lived with her parents.

Zach finds himself attracted to her, just as they had predicted. This girl, who lost her blankie in the rainforest the same night he did all those years ago.

Tom recounts how his parents said that when he was little he lost his teddy bear one night on the treetop walk and the next day they found it sitting on a rock. They told him they thought it very strange that there were other parents and babies out looking for lost toys on that same day also.

The other volunteers pitch in excitedly with their stories. They are all astounded to discover that every one of them had lost a toy or blankie on the same weekend up on the mountain, and all of them feel the same longing to be near or in the rainforest. To protect it. To educate others. To preserve it and its unique flora and fauna. The bond between them is immediate.

Zach senses the sprites' presence, and he turns to see them peering through the foliage. He winks at them and smiles. They attempt the same, but only manage to blink their large emerald-green eyes before drifting off into the night.

Zach is the only one of the group to have met these gentle sprites. After the initial shock of seeing them the first time, and finding out their sneaky little plan, he grew to love them. He was assured that the enchanted Sammie had only instilled in him a love for nature and the ability to pass on that love to others. He'd voiced his concern about the fact that theirs was just one small team protecting one rainforest. What he heard Foster say next astounded him.

'Fairy folk have been performing similar enchantments on human children globally. Wherever there are trees, there are spellbound people such as yourselves working to save the environment. It will gain momentum exponentially'—Foster is proud of his grasp of the human language—'and the shift will bring a halt, in time, to all destructive activities, such as deforestation, mining and general overuse of precious resources. You will find that your presence and your speech is enough to change the thoughts of any opposition. Use it to communicate with your countries' leaders and those with authority or money. All your offspring will be born with the same caring qualities, perhaps more so. You and the following generations can save the earth.'

Zach's thoughts return to the present time. Content, he gazes across the short distance into Chloe's amber eyes.

His heart flips delightedly as she rewards him with a seductive smile.

'A job well done, I believe, Zanna,' Forest says. 'Zach and his future wife, Chloe, will be reliable caretakers of our rainforest. They will have ample assistance from the other recruits and future generations.'

Forest is holding Zanna's delicate slender hand. They dance into the night sky with movements resembling those of graceful ice skaters. A trail of luminescent sparkles is left floating in the cool air behind them.

Zanna has a look of wistfulness as they approach their mountain-stream home. 'It is time for us to procreate, Forest. Perhaps we can get our child one of those odd blankie things that human children have such an attachment to.'

'I think you have spent too much time studying the humans.' Forest is amused by Zanna's comments. 'But, yes, I believe it is time to bring a baby sprite or two into this world, and we can see about one of those blankies, too.'

They frolic in the stunningly clear waterfall, which has taken on a lilac glow in the light of the full moon. Their leader, Avery, and other fairy folk have gathered to play, too, safe in the knowledge that their lush, foliage abundant and life-giving world is protected.

RAINFOREST HEALING

Renee Hills

When the butterflies enveloped her in a million powdery wings, caressing her eyelashes and whispering around her arms and legs, Tabitha thought she was dreaming. How else could she explain the awe and wonder of being surrounded by so many ethereal beings? She blinked and rubbed her eyes. It made no difference— she was still standing in a kaleidoscope of butterflies. They fluttered and wafted on the breeze, an unceasing shimmer of colour and movement.

She deliberately slowed her breathing, lest she inhale a gossamer wing. Her heart steadied its frantic racing. Her legs trembled in the aftermath of the headlong dash into the rainforest. She'd run and run and run to escape the ruinous pain, shame and confusion, and the muisti. She listened for any sound of pursuit; there was only the thumping in her chest and the muffled thud of her bare feet on deep leaf litter. Now she felt the soft swish of the butterfly wings and heard the distant chitter of a small bush bird. Nothing else. Was she safe? Perhaps they'd lie in wait for her in the future. Perhaps they thought she'd be forced to reclaim them. Perhaps she'd never speak of them again.

When her breathing slowed a little more, her vision cleared again. The butterflies hovered and wafted in formation like an effervescent shapeshifter. Tabitha stared at them intently. The details of colour and intricate design on their wings enchanted her, and for a moment she was floating with them, fluttering in the blue, dancing through the treetops, inhaling the oxygen-enriched air, looking down on her frightened self alone on the path. As she flew with them, she saw through half-closed eyes that the shapes and colours on the fluttering wings formed letters of the alphabet, and the words *healing ... healing ...* flashed and blinked over and over again.

She could use healing. Her feet touched the ground again. The butterflies seemed to be inviting her to leave the path and follow the distant sound of softly gurgling water. The butterfly cloud clustered and hovered around a huge cut tree trunk some distance from where she stood. She stepped carefully through small ferns and past massive dangling twisted vines. There was a sudden flurry and lift of wings as she approached, then the butterflies settled again. The rich smell of old wood gently returning its nutrients to the air and earth welcomed her as she peered inside the space.

The trunk's massive diameter meant she could easily stand in the cavity, and she realised she could hide there and escape the notice of anyone or anything on the path. The cavity extended a long way, like a tunnel that offered further concealment. She moved deeper into the trunk, feeling her way in the increasingly dim light. There were weathered wood fragments underfoot and ancient wood rings wrapping around her. She knew this tree must have stood for centuries before it fell and the forest keepers cut the trunk away from the path. Suddenly she stepped into emptiness, and she was spinning and falling, spinning and falling, as if suspended on a silken rope from a giant circus top.

Her feet landed on a flat green swathe. All her limbs and joints seemed okay, and the butterflies were dancing again. That must have been one weird cocktail of medication she took last night. The doctor said it would be okay to combine the sleeping pills with the anti-anxiety meds. There was nothing in the side-effects information about falling through space while dangling on a silken cord. Well, anything was better than the reality she'd recently inhabited. And the butterflies were so beautiful; surely they meant no harm, even in a dream.

She wandered across the green, following the sound of trickling water. She could splash her flushed face and wash off the scratches on her arms and legs from where she'd blundered through the thorny hedge that enclosed the house. Already the scratches looked angry and red, and she felt a fire in her skin beneath them. She hadn't thought to use the gate. Come to think of it, she couldn't remember seeing it; the Sheena's gold hedge seemed to have grown in the night and totally surrounded the house.

All she had known was that she had to run, as far away as possible; to outrun the cruel muisti, the black-winged visions that invaded her sleep and pierced her days with sadness. Although she had resolved to banish them, last night they'd been relentless in their persistence, undermining the very ground of her being. At least here in the rainforest, the pure air and vibrant energy of renewal and growth seemed to have given her relief.

Her feet led her closer to the sound of running water, but she could not see the stream. Instead a tall, white-haired woman dressed in a purple cloak beckoned Tabitha to sit on the mound beside her. In this strange world, Tabitha did not think of ignoring her. There was something irresistible and commanding about her presence, which also radiated kindness and compassion. The butterflies hovered over her.

Tabitha folded her scratched bare legs beneath her and saw they were sitting beside an ancient stone well, its sturdy stone windlass arch now sunken beneath centuries of deposits. Clear water trickled down the stone-lined walls and fell into the deep pool below. Tabitha's mouth and throat were dry and she craved a drink.

The older woman reached out a silver bucket. 'Drink,' she said. 'I drew water when I knew you were coming.'

'You knew I was coming.' Tabitha was amazed. 'Even I didn't know I was coming. I literally fell through a hole to get here.'

'Oh yes, I've been waiting for you,' said the silver-haired woman. 'My name's Saggezza. Welcome to the Well of Tears.'

'The Well of Tears?'

'Yes, surely you are familiar with it.'

'Well, yes ... but I didn't expect to find it here. It's one of the things I've been running from.'

'Dear one, you can never actually leave it behind. You must know that by now. And here are your muisti as well.'

Saggezza pushed a large black velvet bag towards Tabitha, who shrank away in horror.

'No,' Tabitha implored, pushing the bag away with frantic hands. 'No, I've just spent hours outrunning them in the rainforest. I thought it was the running that did it, but now you've got them all collected here in your bag. How did you do that? How can you be sure they're mine?'

'They belong to you, my dear. I should know. I've watched you accumulate and create them all your days. I've marvelled at the sheer tenacity of spirit that's kept you going, despite their fierce teeth and the claws that scratch and irritate you.' Saggezza's voice had softened.

Tabitha looked at her in wonder. Who was this woman who seemed to know so much about her? But Tabitha trusted her implicitly, despite the awful bag of muisti she had captured.

'I can help you with the muisti,' Saggezza said quietly. 'Take my silver bucket.' Her blue eyes twinkled and her rough hand warmed Tabitha's as she handed over the handle of the small ceremonial bucket. It felt cool, yet soothing in Tabitha's fingers.

'First we take out the muisti, one by one,' Saggezza said. 'They're sleeping at the moment, so we lay them out quietly so as not to disturb them, like this.' She spread a ragged, ugly thing on the green. 'Take a long, long look, Tabitha, for this is the last time you will see this muisti. Recall the events that brought this creature into being. And remind yourself that through it all, you always did the best you possibly could, given the information and understanding you had at the time. Now take the bucket. Go to the Well of Tears and collect some water.'

Tabitha obeyed.

'Now pour the water over the muisti,' instructed Saggezza.

Tabitha tilted the bucket and the sad water splashed down onto the creature, dissolving every remnant into the warm earth, leaving only a damp stain.

'Repeat,' said Saggezza, as she carefully laid out another muisti.

Tabitha collected more water and poured. As before, the muisti dissolved.

'Repeat,' said Saggezza.

Soon, the velvet bag was empty, and Tabitha felt freer and lighter than she had done for years.

Saggezza smiled at Tabitha's wonderment. 'You always had the power to do this. I've just shown you a quicker way.'

Tabitha nodded. She didn't trust herself to speak. Her heart expanded with love and gratitude for this mystical being who had just released her from a lifetime of muisti. She never wanted to leave the woman's side.

'You can find me anytime,' Saggezza said. 'The butterflies are waiting. They'll take you home. Keep the silver bucket. You know what to do with it.'

Tabitha felt the soft force of a million powdery wings wafting her above the green, and the Well of Tears.

Saggezza smiled and waved. Around the woman's feet, on the patches of earth made damp by the dissolved muisti, dozens of bush violets pushed through the earth and also waved their smiling faces.

THE SIX

Sarah Hegerty

Milvyre rushed towards the entrance of the trail, skittishly checking behind her to make sure no one had followed. She vividly remembered what had happened to the last elf who was followed to the Gathering, and they were a full member of The Six. Milvyre was still only an apprentice, and a half-blooded elf at that. There were already enough questions about whether she belonged without adding another reason for exile.

Once she had reached the relative safety of the lush rainforest canopy, Milvyre reached into her pack and pulled out her cowl. She threw it over her shoulders as she weaved through the trees, dodging the exposed roots with the grace and speed of a full-blooded elf. As she pulled the rich burgundy hood up over her head, she became just another apprentice, her otherness hidden beneath the cowl.

The Six would still know what she really was, they knew everything. She hoped it wouldn't go against her being selected for a Cluster, and that the Elder Tree Spirits would see her soul was elven, even if her outward appearances was not entirely so.

She had worked hard for this; she deserved to be a Three, the title given to Cluster members of The Six bonded with the Third Tree Spirit.

When she arrived at the Elder Tree, she could see that the summoning fires had already been lit. She was late, again. Another disadvantage of being only a half-blooded elf meant she was cursed to live in the human domain, with human responsibilities. Like having a job. Her blood was not pure enough to become a citizen of the Sacred City, not by their standards. Once she became a member of The Six though, everything would be different. Spell Weavers of The Six were selected by the Tree Spirits, an honour that transcended purity of blood.

The Six was made up of the Chosen, who were standing in front of the summoning fires in their black cowls, their faces painted with coloured clay paint that represented their number affiliation within their Cluster. Other than their different-coloured faces, they were indistinguishable from each other as they faced the apprentices, looking like echoes of a single being.

Ara, one of the Elder Threes, stepped forward and held her hand in the air, three fingers raised to the sky. The apprentice Threes stood and followed her away from the main gathering, Milvyre included. It was the night of selection for the new Cluster. She hoped to be chosen, partly so she would not have to return to her wretched life. Although she was forced to exist in the human world, they were not forced to accept her. She was different, through no fault of her own, and they would not let her forget it. She did not choose her parents, although at times she wished her parents had chosen not to have her.

Milvyre knelt with her head bowed, in a line with the other apprentices, while Ara paced in front of them in a trance. She was channelling the Third Tree Spirit, asking it to choose a worthy apprentice for the next Cluster. A Cluster was formed when each of spirits of The Six chose an apprentice to become bonded to them. It was why they were called The Six: they embodied the power of the six ancient tree spirits.

The compatibility assessment for bonding to a spirit was an arduous process each apprentice undertook before receiving an invitation to the gathering. But compatibility to bond with a spirit did not guarantee compatibility with the Cluster, or that the spirit would desire to be bonded to an individual. This was why the spirits of The Six chose the members of the Clusters, and why the bonding ritual was performed at the Gathering.

Milvyre did not understand the finer details about what that entailed, just that it meant she would be permitted sanctuary in the Sacred City, the place where she was raised. She desired to be chosen with all her heart, so much so that it pounded against her ribcage in a tribal song to the Tree Spirits. And they must have heard, because Ara tapped Milvyre on the head. The sensation was ecstasy beyond anything she had ever experienced. Through that single touch, the Third Tree Spirit channelled its own song, the song that awoke the spell-weaving ability of The Six in her.

Milvyre stood, letting Ara smear the orange conductive paint over her face before moving to the summoning fire with the other chosen apprentices. Together, they faced the flames, reaching out to lock hands with each other, forming a closed loop to contain the energy. As she watched the smoke billow up from the eerie magenta flames, a strong scent of willow wafted through the air. If they were not compatible, this was when they would be taken, a sacrifice of their soul to sustain the elven magic.

Everyone thought Spell Weaver magic came from the forest, and in a way it did, just not in the way most believed. The magic came from elven souls, something only The Six and the apprentices understood. They also understood the need to keep this knowledge close to their hearts because their own people might begin to fear them if they knew the truth. If Milvyre did not have to go back to the humans, she did not care. She would keep whatever secrets she needed to for a chance to belong.

The High Elder, Nueleth, started the bonding ceremony, singing to the forest a mesmerising song that expanded in Milvyre like the universe. It created a feeling of euphoria so deep she wasn't sure she could contain it much longer.

But halfway through the song, voices called out, interrupting the ceremony.

'Stop them. Soul magic is wrong. Stop them.'

Milvyre turned away from the fire to see where the screams were coming from. A tall skinny man—a human in a grey suit and a black tie—stepped through a copse of bushes, waving a baseball bat aggressively in one hand and a book in the other. Behind him, more humans crashed through the bushes holding bats, crowbars, axes, pipes, and other random things that could be used as weapons. They looked out of place in the forest, especially with their aggressive mannerisms and choice of clothing.

Milvyre recognised some of them from when they would mutter hurtful words under their breath as she walked past them in the street—words to remind her she was not one of them. It was part of the reason she had started to wear beanies, to hide the otherness they disliked so much, to try to belong.

A feeling of dread crawled through Milvyre. Could they have followed her to the gathering? Was this her fault? She turned back to the flame and made herself smaller, hoping the intruders would not recognise her.

The other members of The Six created an elven shield, protecting Milvyre's Cluster from the onslaught. The bonding ritual could not be interrupted, and the Elder Tree had to be protected at all costs. Unfortunately, the spirits were tied up with the ceremony, unable to lend their power to the other members of The Six, forcing them to wait until the ritual was complete before allowing them to harness the magic.

Milvyre winced as she watched her soon-to-be kin take a brutal beating to protect her. A helpless guilt began to consume her when she should have been focusing on the ritual.

Suddenly, she felt her soul being torn from her body, and fragments being entwined with shards of the Third Tree Spirit. She collapsed to her knees at the same time as the others in the Cluster. The searing pain coursing through her body was almost enough to cause her to black out. She could feel the forest now, had somehow connected to it.

Somewhere, lost in the blinding agony that crushed them, their consciousness began to merge. With the merging, the undercurrent of raw power threatened to tear their mortal bodies apart. The six spirits rose out of the flames, entwining themselves with each other, ethereal serpents whose colours matched their chosen, becoming a rainbow pushing up further toward the forest canopy above.

The serpents morphed into an abomination without true form, loosely taking on the shape of a giant human. Milvyre, still aware of her own consciousness, also felt the merged consciousness occupy the creature, controlling it. A strange sensation of disconnection washed over her as she watched the abomination taking on her unique features. *Why me?* No one replied. It was as if their consciousness had merged entirely, leaving nothing of themselves. What made her different to the others?

One of the men with a crowbar called out to the monster, 'Hey, it's that half-blood girl from town.'

'Leave,' the monster boomed in an otherworldly voice that shocked Milvyre.

'I knew you were trouble. Stop them,' the man screamed before swinging his crowbar into the monster. The man's jaw slackened, and the crowbar fell to the ground at his side. He looked down at his hands in time to see them dematerialising and being sucked toward the Elder Tree. He started to scream, but the sound was carried away by the wind.

After this, most of the intruders turned and ran, fleeing to protect themselves, except for a defiant few.

One young man who had somehow slipped through the line of The Six cried out before swinging his axe, sinking the blade deep into a vein of the Elder Tree. The Third Tree Spirit was ripped from the monster and sucked back toward the Elder Tree, an orange vapour smeared across the air like a corrosive mist. The severed vein started to rot, a black tar-like substance oozing from it with sickening slowness. A pungent odour of decay began to fill the forest.

All the Threes crumbled to the ground before disintegrating and being sucked into the Elder Tree themselves, just like the Third Tree Spirit, but weaker, as if only a mere shadow of the spirit itself. As the tree absorbed this orange essence, the rot began to spread further, extending out across the ground and into the surrounding trees.

Milvyre felt a sense of loss so great that tears flowed freely from her. She could not understand why she had been left behind, why the tree had not taken her with her kin. She watched in a daze as the chaos continued around her, the other members of The Six moving quickly to neutralise the remaining intruders. Not many remained.

When they were finished, the High Elf approached Milvyre. 'How dare you bring this upon us.'

'It wasn't me,' Milvyre pleaded.

'They knew you, and you live amongst them.' She spat the words in disgust. 'Who else could it have been?' She ripped the cowl from Milvyre's shoulders and threw it into the embers of a summoning fire. 'Be gone and never return,' she bellowed.

'Please,' Milvyre whimpered. 'Let me sacrifice myself to the Elder Tree.'

The High Elf scoffed. 'If it had wanted you, it would have taken you when it took the others.' She pointed into the forest, which had become an entwined fusion of living and dead, to where the humans had come from. 'Just leave.'

As Milvyre slowly pulled herself back to her feet, she saw the others watching her. She noticed someone with a blue face, a One, watching her with calculating eyes. The One's cowl was pulled back exposing her halfling ears, just like Milvyre's own. The One must have noticed Milvyre watching her, because she quickly pulled the cowl back over her head to hide her otherness. Milvyre wondered why she would do that. After all, she was a member of The Six, and her title transcended her heritage.

She watched as the half-blooded One moved away from the group to the remains of the man who had killed the Third Tree Spirit. All that remained was his axe, wallet and some other random trinkets; the rest had been taken by the Elder Tree. She opened the wallet, pulled out a picture and started to weep. Withdrawn into her cowl, it was difficult for others to see her tears, but her body language gave her away.

Milvyre felt like someone had plunged a knife into her heart. How could she have been betrayed by another half-blood, someone who should have understood her better than anyone else?

Recognition hit Milvyre, and uneasiness washed over her. The memory of seeing the intruders before came flooding back, and in that image she saw, standing with them, the half-blooded One, although before now her the One's had always been covered and Milvyre had assumed she was human. They were part of a group that frequented an underground bar called Pure, although from Milvyre's experiences it was anything but.

Milvyre trod through the forest, back toward the human dominion, each rotted tree a painful reminder of what had happened there that night. Thoughts raced through her mind as she plotted the different ways she could make everything right again by exposing the true betrayer of The Six.

YOWIE ON THE MOUNTAIN

Paul Smith

Bath and Baily Investigations would have to do without Harry Bath for three days. I'd planned this trip to Lamington National Park for months, and I was inadvertently about to work on one of the strangest cases I had ever tackled in my long career.

It was nearly a three-hour drive to get to O'Reilly's Resort, where I was going to be picked up. O'Reilly's came to fame back in 1937, when Bernard O'Reilly led a team of bushmen through the rainforest and rescued survivors of a plane crash. And in the forty-odd years since that crash, holidaymakers had flocked to the area. Apparently the area I was visiting was a much quieter side of the mountain. Not many had trekked that path since the original search party.

Professor Higgins had invited me to join him on an archaeological dig, where he had found fossils from a creature thought to be a myth. Higgins probably thought he owed me something for extracting his daughter from a religious cult in Queensland. That assignment nearly got me killed and left lots of unanswered questions when the cult leader was found with a 44-calibre slug in his head.

A purposeful-looking Land Cruiser pulled up, driven by an old Aboriginal bloke named Billy. As we bumped around on the rough bush track, he told me his people shunned this area because of a legendary creature, the Yowie. His people believed the land it inhabited was in the Dreamtime. I didn't fully understand what he meant, but it sounded like a nice spooky tale to scare the tourists.

The dig site lay draped in the shadow of Yarrabillgong Falls. Three camper vans, a couple of tents and a large shade sail made up the complex, next to the recent excavations.

Higgins came out and greeted me, shaking my hand vigorously. 'Harry, you got to come and see what we've found. This is probably the most important discovery of the last fifty years.'

The fossil turned out to be a large humanoid skull with two fangs protruding from the lower jaw. The normally reserved professor was so excited he was shaking.

'This find changes all the known theories of prehistoric creatures in this country. This, Harry, is a skull from a Yowie.'

Despite my recent education from Billy, I knew these beasts were myths and nothing more.

We were interrupted by the arrival of a large beefy bloke with curly red hair and an even redder face. He introduced himself as Hans Kurtz, Higgins' assistant. His guttural accent gave him away as a South African, and I must admit I took an instant dislike to him. My feelings were confirmed by the way he ordered the local lads around. After all, this was their bloody turf.

We spent the rest of the day carefully uncovering fragments of ancient bones, and Higgins became even more excited.

'These bones back up the find and prove beyond a shadow of a doubt that the skull was not planted here.'

Everyone except Kurtz worked like dogs, instead, he seemed to take great delight in handing out instructions. The way the arrogant bastard talked to the three Aboriginal guys was appalling, and I finally told him off in no uncertain terms. When he called me a 'nigger lover' I would have decked him if it hadn't been for Colin holding me back. The South African bloke could obviously handle himself. He was six feet tall, with broad shoulders, and going by the scars on his eyebrows he'd gone a few rounds in the ring.

'Why do you let him get away with that? I asked Colin.

'This find will be good for our people, and we need Kurtz to make it happen.'

'Fair enough.' But I had my doubts.

That night, after a surprisingly good dinner, we sat on fold-up chairs around the campfire, drinking tea. This was a dry work site, so black tea was as strong as it got. I asked Billy, the elder, about the history of the area.

Billy was a natural storyteller, but the one that really got my attention was the legend of the Yowie. Billy had piqued my interest on the drive in, but now I was enthralled, listening to tales of entire tribes wiped out for not respecting the laws of the land. He told the story with so much passion I started to believe it and knew I would probably dream about being torn apart by some ferocious fanged creature.

I didn't dream of monsters, but I was rudely awakened at sunrise by Billy. He was distressed and pale. 'You must come. The professor is *dead*.'

I entered the work-site tent and was confronted by a grizzly sight. Murder makes up a big part of my occupation, but this almost turned my stomach. Higgins lay in a pool of glossy blood, his head smashed in and his chest ripped open. The wounds looked like claw marks.

'Yowie, he come back,' Billy said. 'Him not happy with us digging him up.'

I wasn't entirely convinced, so I scanned the tent for clues. Sure enough, the fossil skull was missing. It had to be worth a fortune, and this whole 'animal attack' scene seemed way too convenient for my liking.

As I left the tent, I spotted Kurtz climbing out of his van. He demanded to know what the fuss was all about.

'Professor Higgins has been murdered,' I told him briskly. 'I'm calling the police. No one is to leave the site.'

He shook his head, as if in disbelief. Then a young Aboriginal girl followed him out of the van, obviously disorientated and I saw that her eyes were dilated. The distinct odour of cannabis wafted through the air.

Seeing the rage that came across Billy's face at the sight of the girl, I figured this was his daughter.

Billy was only half Kurtz's size, but he charged at him, yelling, 'You *bastard.*'

The big man easily fended off Billy's attack, punching him to the ground, then added the boot along with a barrage of disgusting insults. I tore him off Billy, only to be rewarded by a wild haymaker that luckily whistled over my head. I drove my knee into Kurtz's ample stomach and followed it with a driving elbow to his face.

He hit the ground, spitting out blood and possibly a tooth, and wisely decided to stay there. It took every bit of self-control I had to stop myself from getting stuck into him with my own boot.

A young man helped Billy up and took him under the shade sail to clean him up.

Reception was patchy, so it took some time before I learned that CID in Beaudesert would send someone to investigate the murder, but it would take them another few hours to get here.

The flies and stench were nauseating, so I decided to have a look around for clues outside Higgins' tent. Forty-odd years as a PI had taught me to look for anything that seemed out of place. The first thing I noticed was that the spare tyre on the back of one of the campervans didn't match the rest of the van's tyres. It looked more like one off a four-wheel drive.

While I was searching the ground outside the campsite, I spotted a patch of recently disturbed dirt near a tall beech tree. Thirty seconds of digging uncovered a piece of bloodstained wood, with four-inch nails embedded in the knobby end. This had to be the murder weapon.

So much for the Yowie legend.

I was still musing on whether the killer was actually trying to frame a mythical creature when I was hit from behind. I fell flat on my face, still conscious but dazed. Six men, led by a curly-headed bloke in a leather jacket, trudged toward me.

'Hey.' I raised a hand, appreciative of having some help.

Without even looking at me, they walked past, as if searching for something; I swear to this day that the last man stepped right through me. As I was struggling to my feet to follow them, I spotted the leader drop something shiny. I looked down at where it fell, back up again, and … they were gone. Vanished into thin air. Instinctively, I picked up the silvery item and shoved it into my pocket.

I staggered back to camp and heard an engine start up. Sure enough, a four-wheel drive was disappearing into the scrubland. I found the young man I had asked to keep an eye on Kurtz trying, unsteadily, to get back onto his feet. Blood was streaming from the back of his head. No prizes for guessing who the culprit was.

I'd been leery of Kurtz all along. There wasn't much point in trying to pursue him, as all we had at our disposal were the campervans. Besides, Billy told me that Kurtz had a rifle and I had no doubt that he would use it.

It was after midday by the time the police Land Cruiser and ambulance arrived. By then, the flies and smell were more than I could handle. Detective Sargent David Gundu Pa introduced himself. He was dressed in jeans, plaid shirt and RMW boots. In his mid-thirties and of medium height, he looked like he, too, had gone a few rounds. I filled him in on the events of the day without offering my conclusions. It wasn't necessary; this bloke was no dill and knew his business. Anyway, it was pretty cut and dried, especially since Kurtz had done a runner.

Within fifteen minutes they were loading the body into the back of the ambulance and it took off, followed by a swarm of flies.

Gundu Pa approached me and said, 'You're no stranger to this sort of thing. You an ex-cop?'

'Nah, private.' I handed him my card.

'So, what's your read on this?' he asked.

'The skull was worth a fortune. Kurtz killed Higgins, letting the legend of some mythical creature muddy the waters. When Kurtz thought that I was onto him, he bolted, leaving Billy and me with sore heads.'

'He must have known we'd nail him when we found the skull in his possession.'

'Yeah, if you find him, I reckon it was hidden in the spare-tyre cover.'

'I've got Beaudesert Station alerting all nearby towns and resorts. We'll find him, probably bailed up in the bush.'

A few days later David Gundu Pa phoned me at the office to tell me they'd found the vehicle and the skull. There was no sign of Kurtz, but there were bloodstains and footprints of a very large animal dragging something towards Yarrabillgong.

'Where's the skull now?'

'Station,' Gunda Pa replied.

'You might want to put it back where Kurtz's men found it.' I'm not superstitious, but heck, why take chances?

Half an hour later I was sorting out my washing, and out from a pair of cargo pants dropped a silver cigarette lighter. The item I'd seen that trekker drop. The inscription read: *Bernard O'Reilly 1937.*

CONTRIBUTORS

CHARMAINE CLANCY is an Australian author and educator. She is Co-host and sometimes Presenter for the Rainforest Writing Retreat.

When not explaining the dangers of underestimating a fairy or the best spots to hide a body, Charmaine also hosts creative writing clubs for children and produces online workshops for the classroom. As a teacher of literacy, Charmaine encourages children to engage with reading and writing through laughter and exploration. Her own books include *My Zombie Dog, Dognapped? A Dog Show Detective Mystery* and *Undead Kev.* She has won awards for her short stories and is published in anthologies, including the Oz Tales series, *Joe Vale's Last Case,* Short Stories of Mystery and Murder, *Paradigm Shift* in Short Stories of Forest and Fantasy, *Alone in the Dark* in Short Stories of Ghosts and Graves.

Charmaine loves all things Agatha Christie and is often watching those around her with suspicious eyes; on the off chance they ever do commit a cleverly devised crime.

You can find Charmaine at
www.charmaineclancy.com

CHRIS RADGE, is an Australian novelist based in Brisbane, Queensland where she writes fulltime and is a part-time stay-at-home NanMa.

Her published works include in the Oz Tales series, *Smithy*, in Short Stories of Mystery and Murder, *Tinsel Fructify* in Short Stories of Forest and Fantasy, *Ghost Writer* in Short Stories of Ghosts and Graves. Also WAG, *Feathered Hooves* in From the Edge.

She is currently engaged in writing an Octology of YA Urban Fantasy books called the *Elder Scale Series* and two Children's picture books *Where the Lost Things Go* and *Sneezes* that will soon be in publication. A series of ten Tenpin bowling picture books is also in the works as this is another passion having represented Qld for eleven years.

She is a member of Queensland Writers Centre, Booklinks, Australian Fairy Tale Society and looks forward to the **Rainforest Writing Retreat** every year catering for morning and afternoon tea. She has written a 300 page recipe book called *'Nothin to it'* full of easy fifteen minute recipes for the young ones when they venture out into the big wide world.

Chris is a NECA & BICSI multiple award winning non-fiction writer for both Queensland and Australia. A previous editor for a Medical Association Magazine and editor, publisher and marketer for a well renowned Cloth Doll Designer distributed worldwide.

She loves being busy. Lucky hey.

You can find Chris at
www.chrisradge.com
chris.radge@bigpond.com

MARTII MACLEAN lives in a tin shack by the sea, catching sea-gulls which she uses to make delicious pies, and writing weird stories. She likes going for long bicycle rides with her cat, who always wears aviator goggles to stop her whiskers  blowing up into her eyes as they speed down to the beach to search for mermaid eggs.

Martii writes fantastical, adventurous tales for children and teens, and sometimes adults. She lives in Brisbane with her husband Trevor and her cat Minerva. Her work as an educator and librarian, allows her to share her love of books and story-telling with young people and this inspires her to write stories that explore the wonderful world of *'what if'*, including: *If I Die Before I Wake, We of the Between, Unreal Time, Weird Weirder Weirdest, Creepy Creepier Creepiest and The Adventures of Isabelle Necessary.*

She is also featured in Oz Tales, *Mile High* in Short Stories of Mystery and Murder, *The Clockwork Prince* in Short Stories of Forest and Fantasy, *Two Glasses* in Short Stories of Ghosts and Graves.

You can find Martii at
www.martiimaclean.com

FRANK PREM has been a storytelling poet for forty years. When not writing or reading his poetry to an audience, he fills his time by working as a psychiatric nurse.

He has been published in magazines, e-zines and anthologies, in Australia and in a number of other countries, and has both performed and recorded his work as 'spoken word'.

Frank has published two collections of free verse poetry – *Small Town Kid* (2018) and *Devil In The Wind* (2019).

He and his wife live in the beautiful township of Beechworth in northeast Victoria (Australia).

You can find Frank at
Author Page: https://FrankPrem.com
Facebook: https://www.facebook.com/frankprem2
YouTube: https://www.youtube.com/channel/
UCvfW2WowqY1euO-Cj76LDKg
Goodreads: https://www.goodreads.com/author/
show/18679262.Frank_Prem

GEORGINA BALLANTINE, spends her days as a professional editor and author, working her magic on words and whimsy. When not chasing after her three spirited preteens, a paranoid dog and two vampire cats, she hides in her cupboard under the stairs, writing myth-based historical fantasy for adults and children. The opening of her alternate history/fantasy novel-in-progress *Foxfire* won the 2017 CYA Conference Prize (YA category).

Georgina has over twenty years' experience in the publishing industry as a freelance editor and writer. She co-manages the Australian Science Fiction and Fantasy Writers' Association, convenes a speculative fiction writers group and is a committee member of the Australian Fairy Tale Society.

Her growing short story collection of Oz Tales are, *Bonnie and Clyde* Short Stories of Mystery and Murder, *The Vala Tree* Short Stories of Forest and Fantasy, *Tower 13* Short Stories of Ghosts and Graves.

Georgina holds a BA Honours in Classics (Ancient Greek and Latin) and BSc in Environmental Science and Botany.

You can find Georgina at
Website: http://www.firedrakepress.com/
Facebook: https://www.facebook.com/georgina.ballantine
Instagram: https://www.instagram.com/georginaballantine/

LEA SCOTT, has published three psychological thrillers, *The Ned Kelly Game* (2009), *Eclipsed* (2010) and *One for All* (2013). She acts as Chair of the Queensland Writers Centre and mentors new writers under their 'Writer's Surgery'  program. She has facilitated writing workshops and seminars and appeared at writing festivals throughout Australia and overseas. She has acted as associate editor for a Special Issue of *TEXT Journal of Writing*. Lea is currently undertaking a PhD in Creative Writing and has also published academic research on writing about trauma and the transformative potential of creative writing.

You can find Lea at
www.leascott.com

A small rural Queensland town, surrounded by heritage and dust is where **LR JOHNSON** was born and raised. Always with a mind for storytelling in art, she discovered novels and writing in her early adolescence.

Fantastical worlds and far off places penned by the likes of Tolkien, C.S. Lewis and Raymond E. Feist sculpted her imagination. It was this storytelling influence that led her to change college majors from Graphic Design to Digital Illustration graduating with a Diploma of Visual arts and Jewelry Making expanding too many other artistic fields including sculpture and ceramics. There's little true story in a business logo she says.

But storytelling has always remained a constant love of hers and often her stories began with artwork.

You can find Lucy at
Art: www.deviantart.com/lrjproductions
www.facebook.com/StuffLucyMade/

MARIA PARENTI-BALDEY is an unusual creature. She travels by day to her job. But, before the sun salutes another night, she takes a stroll along a path where no other goes. The sky's inky stains release the night voices who storm towards her.  She's a writer and she can't help it. With phone-note and camera in hand she stills - observes, listens and captures. Her note-taking keeps the voices at bay. Her photos submerge her back into the eerie scenes. Some scenes are chilling, others dreadfully dark. When too many voices come, she shelters behind the concrete buildings, placing her out of hearing's reach. However, she's a writer and can't help going back.

Maria is a primary teacher, public speaker and journalist.

You can find Maria at
Website Blog: https://mariaparentibaldey.com/

ROBERT WALMSLEY-EVANS'
greatest passion is fantasy and science
fiction writing. He is also an exhibiting
photographic artist. Robert draws upon
his British heritage and interest in
ancient history to inspire his writing.

Similarly, his world travels through the Mediterranean,
the Netherlands, the U.K, France and the U.S.A have had
a significant impact on his literary practice. Robert has
been honing his craft at the **Rainforest Writing Retreat** for
the past five years and has gained invaluable learning's
from the masterclasses and the vibrant community that
converge at the retreat. He is currently working towards
his first novel length publication, *The Warriors of Lleuad.*

You can find Robert at
Email: robwe92@live.com.au
Facbook: fb.me/robertwalmsleyevansauthor

PAMELA JEFFS is a speculative fiction author living in Queensland, Australia. She is a member of the Queensland Writers' Centre and has had numerous short fiction pieces published in recent national and international anthologies  and magazines. In 2017 she was nominated for an Aurealis Award in the Best Science Fiction Short Story category and in 2018 released her debut collection titled *Red Hour and Other Strange Tales*.

You can find Pamela at
Website: www.pamelajeffs.com
Facebook: @pamleajeffsauthor
Twitter: @Pamela_Jeffs

RACHEL NIGHTINGALE was a highly imaginative child who used to pretend she was wandering the woods in search of adventure on her way home from school. Once she realised creating stories gave her magical powers she decided to become a writer. She is the author of *Harlequin's Riddle* and *Columbine's Tale*, published by Odyssey Books, and rather unexpectedly, an award winning playwright.

Rachel is currently writing the final book in the **Tales of Tarya** trilogy (which by complete coincidence explores the power of creativity to shape the world) whilst desperately trying to ignore all the other stories clamouring for her attention. She lives in regional Victoria with a very bossy cat, her family, and the cutest dog in the world.

The Tarya Trilogy is about the power of creativity and where it can take you. It was inspired by a quote by Broadway actor Alan Cumming about that in-between place you discover just before you step onstage and enter a different world – a place where anything is possible...

You can find Rachel at
Websites:
www.rachel-nightingale.info
www.odysseybooks.com.au
Twitter: @NightingaleRA / @OdysseyBooks
Facebook:
https://www.facebook.com/TalesofTarya/
www.facebook.com/odysseybooks

CHRISTINE KELLY wrote and completed her first story at the age of eleven. After receiving a responding letter from Isobelle Carmody, she was encouraged to continue creating worlds with her words.

She did not truly appreciate the written word however, until her mother introduced her at the age of seven to The Famous Five written by Enid Blyton.

Her travels around Australia ignited her passion for writing. She grew up with her parents and two younger brothers on remote stations throughout Australia.

In 2006, Christine moved to Adelaide, and in 2007 she won second place in the **Lochie Andison Youth Literary** awards with her poem *National Pride*.

She continues her passion for writing – often writing late into the night – while running a small business with her fiancé and is currently working on her first full-length novel.

DR JUNE PERKINS is a Brisbane-based poet, blogger and children's author, of Indigenous Papua New Guinean and Australian background, raised in Tasmania by Baha'i parents. She utilises multi-arts and multicultural stories to  inspire an enriched sense of belonging and compassion in those who encounter her work. She recently shared Magic Fish Dreaming at the Asia Pacific Triennial Pacific, Summer Program 2019 APT9 and became a member of Mana Pasifika research Institute. She maintains an interest and dedication to promoting diversity in the Australian, Pasifika and Baha'i literary landscapes.

You can find June at
https://gumbootspearlz.org/
https://juneperk.wixsite.com/gumbootspearlz

KATRINA RUTGERS is finally pursuing her life-long desire to write with the goal being of publishing a novel.

Katrina, along with attending the 2018 **Rainforest Writers Retreat**, has completed several on-line writers' courses and is a member of **The Hunter Writers Centre** where she participates in suitable writers' courses. She also gains experience by entering the monthly Furious Fiction with the Australian Writers' Centre.

Uniqueness of work is achieved by Katrina via a quirky mind and use of life experiences.

You can find Katrina at
Email: katierutgers@gmail.com
Facebook: https://www.facebook.com/katrina.rutgers

RENEE HILLS is the author of the children's picture book *Turtle Love*, and regularly writes flash fiction for adults for the Facebook *52 Week Flash Fiction Challenge*. She has been published in *Short and Twisted*, Celepene Press 2017.
She is currently working on a junior fiction novel set in a circus in 1930's Australia. In her writing, she draws on her skills and experiences as a print journalist, secondary teacher, and school counsellor. Renee is also involved in climate change activism and believes that we need to honour and respect the interconnected web of all existence, of which we are a part.

You can find Renee at
https://renaissancerenee.com/turtle-love/
https://www.facebook.com/groups/flashfictionchallenge/#_=_

SARAH HEGERTY is a speculative fiction writer, shift-worker, wife, mum, and adventure seeker and who wants some much needed sleep. Living in sunny Queensland, Australia, she spends her time fantasising about snow-covered  mountains in cooler climates. She has had several short stories published in anthologies and is furiously working toward her first novel publication.

You can find Sarah at
Facebook: www.facebook.com/SarahHegertyAuthor/
Twitter: @sarahhegerty
Instagram: @sarahhegertyauthor
Website: sarahhegerty.com

PAUL SMITH is recently retired and started writing his first novel Walk with the Tiger, not long after. This is the first adventure/thriller book in the Jack Harrigan series set in the seventies. The second and third book in the series are in editing. There will be four more Jack Harrigan stories after these.

Paul has also written two short stories, *Monty & Tomatso*. He is also featured in Oz Tales, *Murder on the Mountain* in Short Stories of Mystery and Murder, and *Yowie on the Mountain* in Short Stories of Forest and Fantasy. Paul's one and only Bush poem is *Jack the Dancer*, set in a country pub back in the 1930's.

Paul is part of the **Rainforest Writing Retreat**'s crew assisting where he is needed from driving buses to making sure everybody has settled in to their accommodation.

You can find Paul at
www.PaulSmithAuthor.com

ACKNOWLEDGMENTS

RWR would like to thank Chris Radge (Christine Titheradge), Charmaine Clancy and Anthony Puttee for their hard work in assembling this Anthology and also the warm staff of O'Reilly's who always treat us more like family rather than customers. Likewise, thanks are also due to the RWR retreaters/authors, without whose work there wouldn't be a book. A big thanks to all the crew at the Self-Publishing Lab previously known as Book Cover Café for the amazing cover layout, editing, typesetting and everything else you do. You can contact them at www.selfpublishinglab.com

And the biggest thanks to Charmaine who thought that a writing retreat would be great idea and has run with it ever since.

> " A great way to relax, meet new friends and develop your writing skills. "
>
> ~Renee

SELF-PUBLISHING AND MARKETING YOUR BOOK JUST GOT SIMPLER

selfpublishinglab.com

 ## Online **Classroom**

The Lab is packed with in-depth, step-by-step practical video lessons, tools and resources on preparing, producing, publishing and promoting your book. PLUS the 24/7 community and coaching you need to ensure you achieve your full potential and goals.

 ## Book **Creation**

Let us take care of these one-off tasks, so you can avoid any headaches. Our team is ready when you are. The Lab is an award-winning one-stop shop for creating and publishing a quality book with a team of professionals who care. Oh, and you'll have fun doing it too!

 ## Book **Marketing & Coaching**

From Amazon Ads, building email lists to selling at tradeshows, the Lab has you covered. With courses, templates and our online community, all your questions can be answered with the support of the Lab team and other like-minded authors achieving their goals, just like you.

About the **Self-publishing Lab**

The Lab is an award-winning publishing destination helping thousands of writers avoid the traps in publishing and get started on the right foot.

With over 25 years in the publishing industry, Anthony and the team at the Self-publishing Lab continue to help authors become bestsellers, sell thousands of dollars worth of books online, at schools, workshops and to organisations.

Here's what makes the **Self-publishing Lab different**

 No contracts or exclusive agreements that sell your soul. You'll keep 100% royalties and control without it costing you an arm and a leg to publish your book.

 We show you how to use technology to sell more books while you sleep, even if you're a tech newbie.

 Have your book distributed and available for purchase online around the world, at bookstores and libraries in print and e-book.

Contact Us Today

 w: selfpublishinglab.com
e: support@selfpublishinglab.com

 PO BOX 187
Browns Plains, QLD
Australia, 4118

WANT TO WRITE A NOVEL?
DON'T KNOW WHERE TO START

Join us at Australia's favourite writing retreat

LEARN

Immersive workshops, mentoring & publishing tips from International best-selling authors and industry experts.

CONNECT

Find the support you need and new life-long friends who share your passion. Network, laugh and connect.

PUBLISH

Every year, RWR puts out a high-quality anthology only open to Retreaters for submissions.

SECURE YOUR SPOT!

Each year, 50 writers gather at the spectacular O'Reilly's Rainforest Resort in Lamington National Park. Many of our writers have gone ahead to publish their first works because of the ongoing support and guidance they receive. RWR can book out over six months ahead, so get in early and secure your place. Once you have become a Retreater, you'll also be invited to our private mastermind group, meet-ups, extra workshops and qualify to submit to our publications.

www.RainforestWritingRetreat.com

www.ingramcontent.com/pod-product-compliance
Lightning Source LLC
Chambersburg PA
CBHW020143120726
47903CB00007B/2396